GOD
HATES
US
ALL

GOD
HATES
US
ALL

HANK MOODY

with Jonathan Grotenstein

SIMON SPOTLIGHT ENTERTAINMENT
New York London Toronto Sydney

S|S|E

Simon Spotlight Entertainment
A Division of Simon & Schuster, Inc.
1230 Avenue of the Americas
New York, NY 10020

First Simon Spotlight Entertainment trade paperback edition August 2009

SIMON SPOTLIGHT ENTERTAINMENT and colophon are trademarks of Simon & Schuster, Inc.

For information about special discounts for bulk purchases, please contact Simon & Schuster Special Sales at 1-866-506-1949 or business@simonandschuster.com.

The Simon & Schuster Speakers Bureau can bring authors to your live event. For more information or to book an event contact the Simon & Schuster Speakers Bureau at 1-866-248-3049 or visit our website at www.simonspeakers.com.

Designed by Jaime Putorti

Manufactured in the United States of America

20   19   18   17   16   15

Library of Congress Cataloging-in-Publication Data is available.

ISBN 978-1-4165-9823-7
ISBN 978-1-4391-5435-9 (ebook)

To Mom, for taking me to work.

GOD
HATES
US
ALL

1

DAPHNE LOVED SPEED.

Not in the traditional sense: she rarely pushed her weathered Honda Civic past third gear. The race for Daphne lay in the corridors of her mind, long and labyrinthine, and the girl needed her get-up-and-go. Cocaine, when she could afford it; ephedrine-powered nasal decongestants when she couldn't. But she was never happier than the couple of times I'd seen her receive a shipment of *Simpamina*, which was apparently Italian for "seventy-two straight hours of sex, rock and roll, and menial household chores completed with manic gusto." Followed immediately by four hours of paranoid delusions, violent arguments over meaningless nonissues, and, during our final week together, a pair of suicide attempts wrapped around assault with a deadly weapon.

I met Daphne when I returned to the U, a broke sophomore in need of a part-time job. My summer plans to bus tables for the snobs at the Hempstead Golf and Country Club had collapsed when I'd tried to drive a fully airborne golf cart through a plate-glass window. My passenger—a bridesmaid with Stevie Nicks hair who minutes earlier I'd been finger-fucking behind the Pro Shop—was late for her scheduled toast at the wedding on the other side of the window. The ensuing explosion of glass delivered a thrilling end to what had been, up until that point, a brilliantly executed shortcut across the bunkers on Hole 13, improvised with the help of a half-bottle of Stoli, an angry golf marshal in hot pursuit, and the bridesmaid's reciprocating fingers down the front of my pants. We escaped mostly unscratched, thanks to vodka's armor-plating effects, and the talk of pressing charges turned out to be just that. But the job was history. I spent the rest of the summer as an unemployed thorn in my parents' collective ass.

Back at school, I responded to an ad in the student paper: banquet catering. I began the interview with a heavily edited account of my country club experience, but at the urging of my interviewer—a twenty-something peroxide blonde punk rocker and weekend college radio DJ with a killer smile—I kept adding details until we were both rolling on the floor. I won both the job and an initiation into the strange and wonderful world of Daphne Robichaux, a crash course in alternative music, pharmaceuticals, and a lot of sex, with the occasional light bondage. I let her pierce my left ear and learned to play a few chords on the guitar. When I returned home for Christmas, I announced that I was dropping out of school to write music and shack up with my new soul-mate. My mother wept and refused to talk to me for the rest of the break. My father just shrugged. "Save us some money, anyway," he said.

Whether by miracle or cosmic joke, Daphne and I sur-vived a seemingly endless cycle of dustups and were still to-gether the following Thanksgiving. Neither of us wanted to spend it with family—mine was still sore at me, while Daphne claimed to be an orphan—so instead we planned a Long Weekend of Glorious Ingratitude: four days and three nights in Niagara Falls, where we planned to make a point of never using the word "thanks," preferably while doing a lot of fuck-ing in the tackiest honeymoon suite we could afford.

We packed the Civic and backed out of her snowy drive-way, Daphne nearly guiding the car into the mailman. He sneered at us as he handed her a small white box with an Ital-ian postmark.

"Thank you," she blurted at the mailman. He gave her the finger and walked away.

"I'd just like to point out," I said, looking at the shitty Timex my father *hilariously* called my inheritance, "that it took you under thirty seconds to violate our only rule for the weekend."

"You're driving," she said, already scampering over me. In the time it took me to get behind the wheel and pull the car into the street, she'd ripped through several layers of tape, cardboard, Bubble Wrap, and child-proofing to liberate a handful of the Italians. Her eyes lit up as they traced the pill's familiar contours: one half painted a sinister black, the other half transparent to reveal the timed-release payload of tiny orange and white spansules. "*A salut*," she toasted, swallowing one dry.

An hour later we pulled into an abandoned drive-in movie theater near Seneca Falls. She'd already removed her pants and unzipped mine. I barely had time to shut off the ignition before she climbed over the console, sprung my cock from my fly, and pulled her panties aside far enough to take me in. She slid slowly down to the point where our pelvises met.

That was the end of the slow—from then on we were moving to *Simpamina* time. Using one hand to buffer her head against the Civic's low ceiling, I reached down with the other to recline my chair. The seat flopped backward with a bang, its momentum combining with the physics generated by our energetic coupling to start the car rolling backward down a gentle slope. I hadn't thought to secure the emergency brake.

Daphne's eyes widened with emotion. Fear? Arousal? Both? I was experiencing mostly panic as my body slid backward with the car, making it impossible to reach the brake pedal with my foot. Grabbing the passenger seat, I pulled myself through an incline sit-up toward the hand brake, wrapped my fingers around the handle, and jerked hard. We slid another few anxious feet down the icy grass before crashing into a metal post, one of the drive-in's speakers.

Daphne bowed her head and laughed and quickly rediscovered her earlier rhythm. We finished quickly and exited the car to inspect the damage to the bumper, which proved minor. She popped another pill and we were back on the road.

Two hours later, we checked into the Royal Camelot Inn, sold by the availability of the honeymoon suite and the "I came-a-lot at the Camelot" T-shirts on sale in the lobby. We cracked open the complimentary bottle of pink champagne, broke in the Jacuzzi tub, and managed one more ferocious screw in the heart-shaped bed before I collapsed into a dreamless sleep. I awoke eight hours later to find Daphne cleaning the tub, having commandeered a spray disinfectant during her sleepless exploration of the hotel and its surrounding area. She'd already planned our day: a visit to a winery just across the Canadian border.

The region was too cold for traditional winemaking, our tour guide explained—the grapes froze on the vine before they were ready to be harvested. Driven by ingenuity and the desire for drink, the locals had developed a time- and labor-intensive process that squeezed just a few drops out of each icy fruit, the result a thick and sweet concoction called "Ice-wine."

Which we never got to try. While we'd taken the tour as a way to exploit Canada's more kid-friendly drinking age— Daphne was a wise old twenty-two, but I still had a year and a half to go before my twenty-first birthday—Daphne pulled me into a restroom as our group moved into the tasting room.

Our sexual odyssey, however, was taking its toll, specifically on my manhood: the chafing made Daphne's soft and wet feel like an electric power sander. I told her so when, on our return to the parking lot, she unzipped my pants, seemingly intent on giving me head.

"Whatever," she said, jerking the zipper closed. She began to walk toward the area's main event—the roaring Falls—then picked up her speed to a light jog. Soon it was a full-on sprint.

Maybe she wasn't going to hurl herself over the side, I thought as I sprinted after her, ignoring all kinds of pain as my jeans gave my sore groin a good working over. But she sure looked hell-bent on trying. As she neared the edge, I literally leapt for her ankles and pulled her to the ground.

"What the fuck, Daphne?"

My chivalry was rewarded with a flurry of punches to the face and chest. I shielded my face and bucked her off me. I waved at a few gawkers who were pointing in our direction. "We're all right," I yelled. "She's got a medical condition."

We didn't speak the entire drive back to the hotel. As I climbed out of the car, she grabbed the keys and sped away. I returned to the room, where I lay in the bed watching the same highlights on ESPN for almost four hours before she returned.

"I wasn't sure you were coming back," I said.

"Neither was I," she replied. "But I was afraid you'd keep the pills." She retrieved the bottle from the bathroom and helped herself to another.

"You want to fuck yourself go right ahead," I said.

"You already told me that when you rejected me in the parking lot."

I don't remember what else was said that night. The pattern, by now, was familiar: accusations and tears, harsh words, and, eventually, reconciliation. An attempt at makeup sex, cut short by the sorry state of my inflamed penis. We fell into a wordless cease-fire and, finally, a restless sleep.

Or at least I did. When I jerked awake, she was staring at me, bouncing slightly, seemingly full of life. Only her zombie eyes betrayed the fact that she was on her second straight day without sleep. "Number Three," she stated.

Our "Worst Fight Ever" took place just two weeks into our relationship, on our way back from a Meat Loaf concert. Then, a week later at an around-the-world party in my dorm, we fought a sangria-fueled reenactment of the Spanish Civil War. During a recent makeup session we'd listed our Top 5 Fights on the chalkboard in her kitchen, hoping the sight of so much water under the bridge would inspire future harmony. So far, the list had only succeeded in presenting more opportunities for argument, as new battles jockeyed for position with the old.

"Seriously?" I asked, pointing to the bruises on my arm. "Number Two, missie. Might give Number One a run for its money, if there's any scarring."

"Pussy," she said, punching me in the arm.

Neither of us felt like returning to the Falls, and after two days the room felt more prison than escape. We climbed into the car and began the drive back to school. Daphne celebrated the start of our journey with another *Simpamina*.

"Where do you even get them?" I asked.

"From Dino," she replied.

Dino was a Roman she'd dated during a semester in Italy when she was an undergrad art major. He'd been a genius artist, or so she said. I tended to ignore most of what she said about Dino, as in addition to vast artistic talent he'd apparently been endowed with a cock *molto mostruoso* and the equivalent of a graduate degree in Italian lovemaking. While I was generally confident in my own size and skills, talking Dino reminded me that Daphne was our relationship's wiser and wilder elder, making me feel like a groping pretender.

"Ah, Dino," I said. "Your friend with the *Flintstones* name."

"That wasn't funny the first time you said it. Or the six thousand times since." Daphne's spine stiffened for a fight. And I was feeling stupid enough to give her one.

"Dino," I continued. "The genius artist who's what, thirty? And still lives with his parents."

"You know damn fucking well that's the traditional living arrangement in Italy. It's not like the consumerist hell we live in here. Family values actually mean something."

"Just saying. Real geniuses don't live with their parents."

Her response was fast, effective, and very nearly fatal for both of us. She grabbed my arm, pulling me—and the steering wheel—toward her. As I leaned the other way to straighten the wheel, she punched me, without letting go of my arm, around my head and neck as hard and as fast as she could. What she lacked in strength, she more than made up for in speed.

"I hate consumerism!" she screamed.

The car began to spin, slowly, but still precariously out of control. I struggled to restore authority over the vehicle with my free arm while deflecting punches with the other. "I hate consumerism!" she continued to yell again and again, like a chanting monk.

Now we were facing oncoming traffic. Cars swerved past us, their drivers' faces rigid with shock, terror, and fury at an unpredictable universe. I began to smile, the same dumb expression that was plastered on my face when the Civic completed its 360-degree turn and slammed broadside into the center divider.

We sat in the emergency lane, motionless and silent. Until Daphne leapt out of the passenger seat, skirted three lanes of interstate traffic, and disappeared into a snowy copse of trees.

I banged the steering wheel angrily. I had a pretty good case for leaving her here. Let her hitch a ride. She'd get home eventually, full of piss and vinegar and maybe unwilling to ever forgive me, but fuck it: This time our relationship was done. Number Two had become Number One and there was no going back.

I slammed the wheel a few more times, cursing Daphne, Dino, myself, and lastly my parents for being such assholes that I'd had to even take this goddamn trip. Then I unbuckled my seat belt and played a real-life game of *Frogger* across the highway, hoping to find her.

It wasn't very hard. She'd fallen to her knees about thirty yards from the road. I approached slowly, softly repeating her name, trying to get a read on her emotional temperature. I interpreted her silence as welcoming so I moved in, placing a hand on her shoulder. A sharp burst of pain in my own shoulder provided instant feedback as to just how badly I'd misread the situation.

The switchblade was another Italian souvenir, something she began carrying full-time after a female student had been raped on campus. She dislodged the knife from my shoulder. I had time to scream in pain before she stuck me again, this time in my thigh. Then she went for the chest. Some instinct toward self-defense ordered my forearm to push back, flinging her backward almost comically into a snowdrift. I tried to step toward her, but the pain in my leg dictated otherwise. I crumpled to my knees and rolled onto my back, staring at the dark gray sky, bleeding into the snow, waiting to die.

2 DURING THE KIRSCHENBAUM SEDER OF '84,
hopped up on hormones and Manischewitz, I
kissed then-thirteen-year-old Tana Kirschenbaum
while we were supposed to be hunting the *afikomen*. I even
made a run at fondling her breasts—marvelous then, nothing
but improvement since—until, to my great dismay, she shut
me down. It wasn't that Tana didn't like me: She just already
knew better than to trust me. And while I lost a potential
conquest, I found a sister. In the years since, Tana had been
chief strategist to my romantic entanglements. She helped me
make sense of my feelings when love was in bloom and, when
it wasn't, listened patiently to my sins. In return, I offered sage
advice regarding her own affairs of the heart, which tended to
be long on deep, meaningful embraces but short on the
down-and-dirty. "He's definitely gay" was my most frequent
observation.

With the exception of last Thanksgiving—it's hard to believe that a year has passed since my Long Weekend of Glorious Ingratitude—the Kirschenbaums have provided the
setting for most major holidays. My own parents are short on
family ties: Mom's clan of no-nonsense Protestants reside
mainly in her native Indiana, while Dad's relations—to call
them lapsed Catholics doesn't quite capture the length of the
fall—always seem to be engaged in some blood feud preclud-
ing any possibility of face-to-face contact. Larry Kirschenbaum, who's thrice defended my father on charges of driving
under the influence, is the closest thing Dad has to a friend.
Still, my father harbors an abiding suspicion, repeated each
time we pile into the car to go, that the invitation allows Larry
to write off the cost of the meal.

This year's table seats thirteen, which for the Kirschenbaums is an intimate affair. No one is sober enough to retrieve dessert. I'm fairly certain that Dottie, Tana's heavily
mascaraed but otherwise remarkably preserved mother, is
flirting with me. There really isn't any other way to make
sense of her so far unquenchable interest in my current job,
slinging soft-serve at the Carvel on Jerusalem Avenue.

Dottie's stocking foot, now tracing a line up my leg, confirms my theory. Awkward, as I'm sitting next to her husband.
Doubly awkward, as I'm pretty sure Dottie and my father
have engaged in carnal gymnastics on more than one occasion. Sure enough, Dad—who's spent most of the night fix-
ated on Tana's glorious rack—is glaring at me with a look that
might be intimidating if not drowned in scotch. I'm relieved

to see that Mom's too dead-eyed to notice, thanks to Dr. Marty Edelman, an orthodontist whose recent vacation to Napa Valley apparently produced no detail too small or insignificant.

While I can imagine worse fates than sinking my Fudgie the Whale into Dottie's Cookie-Puss, the idea of going where my father's been strikes me as a little too Oedipal for comfort. I excuse myself and step outside for a cigarette.

Uncle Marvin has beaten me to the stoop. He isn't my uncle—avuncularly speaking, he belongs to Tana—but he's as much a fixture at these things as the cloth place mats. A year or two north of sixty, he still sports a full mane of shiny gray hair, less a sign of virility than a cruel reminder. He was one of New York's Finest during the seventies, until six bullets to the legs and groin led to an early retirement, a permanent limp, and a urinary tract fucked up enough to require a permanent piss bag. Tana claims he's supplementing his disability pay with part-time work evicting foreclosures—a booming business thanks to the recent savings and loan scandal—but none of that money seems to have found its way to his wardrobe: polyester pants, long-collared shirt, and a black leather jacket that, like Uncle Marvin himself, has seen better days.

"Uncle Marvin," I say.

Uncle Marvin grunts at me like I'm an idiot. I'm not offended—we've had entire conversations that didn't consist of much more. He watches me bang my pack against the back of my hand for a few seconds before reaching into his jacket for a hand-rolled cigarette and a book of matches. Then he slips a match between two fingers and lights it directly into his cupped hands, which form a natural shelter from the icy wind. A pretty cool trick, I have to admit. As he puffs his smoke to life, I counter by flicking a Zippo twice across my pants leg—not the only thing I learned during my brief college experience, but definitely the most useful. I light the unfiltered Camel and take a deep drag, suddenly noticing an odor even more exotic than my favored blend of Turkish and American tobaccos.

"That doesn't smell much like a cigarette," I say.

"You fucking kids wouldn't know good grass if it smacked you in the eye."

"I've smoked marijuana before," I reply, recognizing that I'm in serious danger of being outcooled by a ball-less old man dressed like Serpico.

"Well, my niece sure as shit ain't."

"I thought we were supposed to 'Just say no'?"

"Not advice," he says, exhaling through clenched teeth, "that would ever come from me."

He offers me a toke, which I decline. "I'm kind of going through a scotch and cigarettes phase right now," I tell him.

"Get it in while you can. It'll all be gone soon enough."

Conversations with Uncle Marvin tend to be short, given his natural aversion toward anything polite, but I'm not in a hurry to get back inside and more than willing to pick up the slack. "I hear you. I'm thinking about moving to the city."

"The city?" His eyes narrow. "Everybody I know is leaving. City's a goddamn cesspool."

"Well, that should make it much easier for me to find an apartment."

"Funny," he says without smiling.

A minute or two pass in silence, which I take to mean our conversation has ended. "Thanks as always for the witty repartee," I say, tossing the butt to the ground and stamping it out with my toe. "I'd better get back inside before my father makes the moves on your niece."

"Wait a minute. . . . When you go into the city, you can pick me up some more." He raises the joint by way of explanation.

"You know I'd love to help you, Uncle Marvin, but I wouldn't even know where to—"

"You go see my guy. Here . . ." He produces a bankroll the size of a baby's fist from his front pocket, peels off six twenties, and presses them into my hand. "That'll buy a quarter."

"A quarter?"

"A quarter ounce. And don't let him dick you with the stems and seeds. Dead weight, that shit."

To be completely honest, I am grateful to have something to do that doesn't involve ice cream.

The next morning, I rise early and dress in the dark, slipping out of the house before my parents can wake up and ask questions. A fifteen-minute walk later I'm aboard the Long Island Rail Road, just another head in the morning cattle drive to New York City. I find a seat next to an asshole in a suit reading the *Journal*. The car bounces gently as the train rumbles past row after row of working-class houses. I'm trying to decide if "working class" is an oxymoron when a frosted blonde in a work skirt sashays past me. While my time with Daphne taught me, among other things, that I wasn't the biggest fetishist when it came to sex, there's something about the combination of stockings and running shoes that does it for me. I spend the next thirty minutes wondering if there's a railway equivalent of the Mile High Club. On reaching the station, the cattle rise to their feet, driven toward the exits by instinct and caffeine. I drift along for the ride, floating on a wave of group dynamics toward Seventh Avenue.

Uncle Marvin's connection is in Alphabet City, making convenient travel all but impossible. The easiest thing would be to hail a cab, but I'm still hopeful that my day as a drug mule might result in a profit. So after some consultation with a subway map, I hoof it a block east, shell out two bucks for a couple of subway tokens, and take the F to Second Avenue. A grizzled wino in a ski cap stumbles through the car, rattling a Styrofoam cup, offering God's blessings every time a straphanger adds a few coins. I feel an urge to shake the guy—what kind of God does he think is watching out for him? I get my answer a minute later, when a second beggar enters the car from the other direction. The flow of donations comes to an abrupt halt. It's as if the sight of so much hopelessness smothers any impulse toward charity. If there is a God paying attention to this pair of lost souls, He's got a wicked sense of humor.

Emerging on Houston Street, I try to match the brisk and focused New York Strut. I don't want to look like a tourist. I turn left (*north*, I remind myself) on Avenue A and pass through Tompkins Square. Newly erected plastic fences keep would-be homesteaders off the grassy parts—and, in the process, everybody else. The end result looks less like a park than a museum to mourn the passing of public space. "Believe it or not," says the imaginary tour guide in my head, "children were once allowed to roam freely on these lawns."

At the park's far corner, a congregation of skinheads causes me to quicken my pace. One of them has a swastika tattooed to his forehead. Good luck getting a job, Fritzie. I don't have to make eye contact to know that they're staring at me, which gets my heart racing, but I'm apparently white enough to earn passage without molestation. While I don't have any idea whether or not Uncle Marvin's notion of a New York exodus is grounded in fact, I'm beginning to see the rationale. The prevailing atmosphere is despair, punctuated by moments of terror.

A block later, I'm in Puerto Rico, or so I'm led to believe by the complete lack of English signage. I stand in front of the address Uncle Marvin gave me, a five-story building anchored by a boarded-shut nightclub that doesn't seem like it will be reopening anytime soon. I buzz Apartment 4D.

"Yah?" crackles the response.

"Marvin Kirschenbaum sent me. I'm looking for—"

The buzzer buzzes and I scramble to push through the door in time. Inside a dimly lit hallway lined by mailboxes, I scan the names until reaching 4D: "The Pontiff." Apparently this is a holy pilgrimage. I look up, drawn by a sudden commotion in the stairwell. Raised voices. A slamming door. A bilingual explosion of English and Spanish curse words.

I begin a cautious ascent, encountering the source of the commotion, or at least a key participant, on the stairs between the second and third floors. He's a kid about my age, Puerto Rican, wearing an oversized Tommy Hilfiger shirt and baggy, low-riding Girbaud jeans, plus scuffless Air Jordans that would set me back what I make in a week at Carvel. Noticing me, he spits on the ground. Then he rips a Motorola pager from the hem of his pants and smashes it against the wall.

"Nothing personal," he says.

I nod and continue without further incident to the fourth floor, where Apartment 4D anchors the end of the hall. I knock on the door.

A peephole slides open, revealing an eye. "You a cop?" growls a voice from the other side.

"No sir," I reply, figuring that even drug dealers appreciate good manners.

The eye blinks two or three times before the slot slams shut. From the other side, I can hear five locks unfasten in succession. Then the door swings open, revealing a second door.

"You packing?" asks the door, which I now recognize to be an extremely large black man in a dark blue warm-up suit.

"I've got cash, if that's what you mean," I reply. My palms are sweating.

"Good for you." Suddenly his large hands are roaming up

and down my body. It's all very clinical and detached, but that doesn't stop me from squirming.

"Keep it up and you're going to have to buy me a drink," I say.

The Man-Door silently ushers me into a room about the size of a high school cafeteria, an illusion enhanced by fluorescent lighting and foldout banquet tables with built-in benches. Only in this alternate universe, high school is populated entirely by middle-aged Puerto Rican women.

The room, while fragrant, doesn't smell anything like a cafeteria. The redolent piles of marijuana that blanket the tabletops make me think of freshly mowed lawns. The women tear off hot dog–sized chunks and plop them on scales, adding and subtracting nuggets to achieve some ideal weight before bagging the results in half-sized Ziplocs I've never seen at any supermarket. A fat man with squinty eyes—this Bizarro school's assistant principal—waddles among the tables, keeping an eye out for any funny business and occasionally replenishing the grass from a more familiar-sized Hefty bag. At least a dozen more such bags form a hill in the room's far corner.

The only other furniture is an old desk in the opposite corner, occupied by a thin man with a wife beater T-shirt and an unlit cigarette hanging from his mouth. The desk's only adornments are a clean-as-new ashtray and a push-button telephone that seems to ring every time the thin man finishes a call. While I'll later learn that, for reasons that should have been obvious, the room is subject to a strict no-smoking policy, in the moment it's hard not to think of Sisyphus, his never-ending task a perpetual roadblock to his nicotine fix. The thin man's job doesn't seem to involve much more than the repeating of addresses, which he inscribes without edits onto Post-it notes and jams onto a subway map tacked to the wall.

"Wake up, boy. The Pontiff is waiting," says the Man-Door. He doesn't waste any additional time with words or gestures—his enormity simply eliminates every option other than a door in the back of the room.

I enter a small room whose only light comes from an honest-to-goodness lava lamp, bathing everything in shades of red. *A lair*, I think, hearing the door close behind me. My eyes slowly adjust, revealing walls and ceilings lined with the kind of batik tapestries that were so popular at college among veterans of prep school and fans of the Grateful Dead. The room's sole inhabitant turns out to be a Caucasian male in his fifties who would have looked out of place anywhere but at a Dead show. There's a small soul patch on his chin and dreadlocks, either bleached or naturally orange, extending halfway down his back. He's dressed like a South American farmer, but everything else about him suggests royalty, from the plush velvet armchair he occupies like a throne to the way he tilts his head, almost imperceptibly, toward the throw pillows that line the room's floor. I recognize the gesture as an order to sit down. Which I do.

The man in the throne—the Pontiff, I presume—peers at me as if I might not be real. "So," he finally declares. "You're the kid."

I nod.

"And you're ready for this." His questions don't have question marks. He's not searching for answers; he's confirming that which he already knows.

"I think so." I reach into my pocket for the money. "Marvin didn't tell me much."

"Marvin."

"Marvin Kirschenbaum." I pick up one of the bills, which I've fumbled to the floor. "He said he wanted a quarter."

"A quarter."

"A quarter ounce?"

"This isn't about the position."

"Marvin didn't tell me anything about a position," I say, hoping my voice doesn't betray what is basically escalating terror bordering on trouser-soiling hysteria. Every instinct in my body demands that I get the fuck out of Dodge. But my mouth, for some ungodly reason, keeps moving: "Could you tell me a little more about it?"

"So you *are* here about the position." The Pontiff turns his gaze toward a small wooden box, although I'm pretty sure he's still talking to me.

I take a deep breath. "I'm not sure I have enough information yet to answer that question."

The Pontiff nods, my fate seemingly decided, and opens the box. It's full of weed. He removes a pinch of his product and crumbles it between his fingers into the bowl of a three-foot-high bong I'd somehow missed. "It was my original understanding," he says, striking a foot-long match against its cylindrical package, "that you were here to replace Carlos. Tell me why I should hire you." He places the lit end of the match next to the bowl and inhales, causing the flame to leap to the powdery grass. The water at the bottom of the bong gurgles as the glass tube becomes opaque with smoke for maybe twenty seconds.

I take a deep breath. *Pull it together, kid.*

"I am twenty years old," I begin, "an age at which they say we're supposed to be figuring it all out. And I'm taking them at their word. Following my heart. Pursuing that which interests me. Satisfying my *wanderlust.* It's a philosophy that so far has led me to the food service industry, which I'll be the first to admit isn't exactly where I'd like or hoped to be, even before certain incidents—one incident, really, a solitary expression of youthful overexuberance—did considerable and more likely than not irreparable harm to my prospects in the trade. Another interest I have pursued is the opposite sex— the females, the ladies—and not to brag but let's just say I've had a little more success than I've had with the food service industry. Good in the sack, or so I've been told. Seriously—I can get references—although maybe not my last girlfriend, who for reasons that are still unclear to me stabbed me with a knife and saddled me with trust issues. Those issues, plus my current job making ice cream cakes shaped like marine life, have led to decidedly fewer encounters with the ladies and, I'm afraid to say, a premature cynicism unbefitting my age."

Only I don't say any of that. Instead, I serve up a couple of platitudes about being reliable and willing to work hard.

"You can keep your mouth shut," says the Pontiff.

I nod yes. Twenty minutes later, I'm walking out of the building with a new job, one that promises relatively high pay and easy work, fuck you very much Tom Carvel. It isn't until I board the train back to Long Island that I realize I've forgotten to buy Uncle Marvin his weed.

3

"MAYBE YOU CAN JUST GET SO SMART THAT YOU don't want to have sex anymore," Tana says. She's wearing a T-shirt and boxer shorts and is bent over into some kind of yoga pose. A class she's taking at school.

"Fortunately I'm not that smart," I say. "Is it customary at Cornell to do yoga in your unmentionables?"

"Nope. For the girls it's mostly Lycra and thongs. Who can we ask who's really smart?"

I sit on her pink desk, studying a collage of handsome pop stars and teen idols that's been tacked to her bulletin board for as long as I've known her. "While it's true I'm no longer a college man, it's been my experience that man developed brains to get *more* sex, not the other way around."

"I mean, Glenn is totally brilliant," she says, breathlessly, although that might be part of the yoga.

"He can't be that brilliant if he doesn't want to have sex with you."

"Says you. His doctorate is on applied semiotics."

"Can't say I'm too familiar with the subject. Now applied *semen*-otics . . ."

"You mock," she says, stretching for her toes, "what you don't understand."

"Welcome to the story of my life."

"You have to listen to him talk about it. I get so fucking hot just hearing who he's reading." She rises and walks toward me, mock-seductive. "Lacan . . . Derrida . . . Foucault." I growl appreciatively and she reconsiders her approach. "So enough about my misery," she says, folding her arms. "Who are you boinking these days?"

"A mouth like a sailor, you."

"Come on, fess up. What about that waitress? The one with the silky blonde hair and the perky tatas?"

"Heidi," I say. A summer fling. We used to hook up after her late shift at Bennigan's, when her silky blonde hair smelled tragically of stale beer and smoke and even her tatas were exhausted. "We hit a point."

"Let me guess. . . . She got tired of being a booty call?"

"Excuse me for not wanting to jump back into a serious relationship."

Tana perks up considerably. "Let me see them again."

I pull down the collar of my shirt, exposing the dime-shaped scar—the one I can show her while keeping my pants on.

"Dag," she says. "Bitch was mental."

"No argument here. But we had our moments."

Tana sighs melodramatically. "And now you'll never fall in love again."

"On the contrary. I plan on falling in love many, many times."

"True love is just a joke?"

"Jokes are funny. True love is not only bogus, it's hazardous to your health."

"Get stabbed by one psycho . . ."

"I'm serious," I say. "Some chemicals in your brain trick you into thinking you've got feelings for someone. And that's when the troubles begin. Let your guard down, and it's like Lucy with the football."

"You're supposed to be cheering me up."

"I thought that I was. Did you not catch the *Peanuts* reference?"

"I think this new job is going to be good for you. At least you'll meet some people you didn't know in high school."

My new job began the morning after my interview. As directed by the Pontiff, I met Rico near the ticket counter at Port Authority. My audition.

The work was, not surprisingly, illegal, but as far as I could tell, relatively low-risk, at least for me. The Pontiff had a system for pot delivery as innovative as it was audacious, allowing desirers of the devil's lettuce to let their fingers do the walking whenever the need arose. An operator was standing by—Billy, the Sisyphus in a wife beater I'd seen at the apartment. One hour later, at a spot near but never too near their location, the happy smokers could trade $100 for what Rico called "a gentleman's quarter." I asked Rico what a gentleman's quarter was.

"A convenience tax," he said.

The operation wouldn't have been possible without that modern convenience: the pager. In a way that I'll admit is not altogether healthy, it's what finally sold me on a job that, had I a gentleman's quarter of moral judgment or common sense, I would have declined. But the Motorola Rico handed to me was a miniature homage to the state-of-the-art: a two-line, forty-character display (a feature Billy stubbornly refused to embrace, never straying from his standard "420"); the time and the date (I would finally get rid of the shitty Timex); eight selectable musical alerts (with strict orders to leave it on *vibrate*—Billy again); and a built-in alarm clock (a good idea in theory; unnecessarily jarring in practice). I felt like James Fucking Bond.

"The tether," Rico called it. Maybe. But after a year of wandering alone in the desert, I was ready to be tethered. Even if it was to an organization of criminal stoners. And for criminals—and more impressively, stoners—they were re- markably well-organized.

The most important part of being a "Face"—the Pontiff's term for what most employers would call a delivery boy—was to maintain a bottomless supply of loose change and subway tokens. The rest of the job was staying near a pay phone, pref- erably someplace warm, and waiting for pages from Billy.

The ensuing conversations were short and to the point: two locations—the Pick-Up and the Meet-Up.

In its own way, the Pick-Up was even cooler than the pager. Billy, using some arcane logic understood only by Billy, directed the Face to what was typically a crowded meeting place. There the Middleman—more often than not Joseph, a wiry Rasta with a scar on his cheek—bumped into the Face, slipping a bag (the gentleman's quarter) into his pocket. The entire interaction went down without greeting or acknowledgment—despite my couple of stabs at subtle nods and raised eyebrows, Joseph seemed intent on taking the "not acknowledging me" part of his job very, very seriously.

In the unlikely event that some eagle-eyed lawman happened to spot the transaction, the bag's small size and the lack of any financial component meant, at most, a Class B misdemeanor, which Rico mentioned in a way that made me think it wasn't very scary. But it never came to that. The city was averaging three murders and God knows how many assaults, rapes, and robberies a day, providing more than enough drama for a police force that was by its own estimation undermanned and overstretched. I'm pretty sure we could have made the Pick-Up wearing clown suits and playing tubas and brooked no interference from the men in blue.

Which allowed the Face a half hour, more or less, to get to the Meet-Up with the customer.

The Meet-Up never took place at the actual spot relayed by Billy. Throughout the first day, I watched Rico walk each prospective buyer to a nearby alleyway or secluded stoop, where he subjected them to a series of questions he later told me were written by the Pontiff's lawyers. "Don't matter how big a hard-on the judge has to put you away," he explained. "A cop answers these questions, that's stone-cold entrapment."

But again, it never came to that. At the end of the shift—a closet traditionalist, the Pontiff broke up the workweek into five eight-hour stints—the Face and the Middleman met for a final bump. This time it was cash that changed hands—the day's take minus the daily wage, which for me was $80.

It may not have been a foolproof scheme, but as long as no one acted like a fool, it might as well have been. Or so said the Pontiff, who promoted his business with a cheekiness bordering on the absurd—not even his most addled customers could forget the toll-free number he provided to them: 1-212-GET-WEED.

My new job.

"I'm a drug dealer, Tana. No one wants to hang out with their drug dealer."

"Good point," she concedes, curling into another yoga position. "I guess you're destined to be friendless and alone, except for me."

"You're going back to school."

"You could always get arrested. Three words for you: Hot. Prison. Sex."

"Don't think I haven't considered it," I say, sliding off the desk. "Speaking of work . . ." I toss her a gentleman's quarter. She opens it and inhales the bouquet. "For your uncle Marvin. Don't pinch too much."

"Uh, I'm leaving tomorrow morning? I'm not exactly going to see him before I go."

"Then give it back."

Tana's face goes pouty. "You don't even like weed," I say.

"I don't. Usually. But Glenn said something about wanting to get high. . . ."

"Why didn't you say so? Consider it my donation to your erotic well-being. I'll get Marvin another bag."

"You see that?" she says, slipping the grass into her makeup bag. "That, my friend, is good karma. You just sit back and watch. The universe is going to reward you."

4

NOT MEETING PEOPLE ISN'T THE ONLY THING standing between me and a social life. There's also the fact that I'm still living at home.

My parents drove to Niagara Falls to pick me up from the hospital. We returned home in relative silence, which was fine by me; at least there weren't any questions about Daphne. By the time we were pulled into the driveway, I'd decided that I could tolerate a week or two under their roof. Just enough time to get me back into the game.

But what game? As my wounds healed and my restlessness grew, I made two disturbing discoveries: (1) the U wasn't in any hurry to take me back, given how badly I'd slacked off during my last semester there; and (2) I was an untouchable, at least as far as Nassau County's food service industry was concerned. The events at Hempstead had turned me into a local celebrity. And while many free drinks flowed my way, the job offers did not. Only my old boss at Carvel, where I worked my senior year in high school, took mercy on me when I agreed to work for minimum wage. Which wasn't going to rent me living quarters that didn't have the name "Projects" attached to it.

I quit Carvel the night I returned from my orientation with Rico. In a couple of weeks, I'll have enough saved up to find a place of my own. Maybe even in the city, like I'd boasted to Marvin.

But I need a story to tell my parents. Too risky to lie about a restaurant job—the city's close enough for a surprise visit. I decide to tell them I've found steady work as an office temp. Which means smiling a lot while my mother, bursting with joy at her newfound ability to use "my son" and "office" in the same sentence, drags me to the mall and forces a whole new wardrobe upon me. And she wakes up early Monday morning to make me breakfast, meaning I damn well have to wear it. I'm pretty sure I will be the only weed dealer in the tristate area rocking business-casual.

By the time I get to the city for my first day flying solo, the pager's already buzzing. "Pick-Up's at the Fifty-Ninth Street Station, near the newsstand. Meet-Up is at the Engineers' Gate, Ninetieth and Fifth Avenue. Young lady. Look for Lycra."

I think I'm going to like this job.

The problem, when I get to the gate, is an embarrassment of riches. Every third or fourth person is a woman under thirty wearing Lycra, Upper East Side runners toning their glutes on the loop around the Central Park Reservoir. My eyes finally settle on the one who isn't running.

She's a few years older than me, maybe twenty-six or twenty-seven. Fair skin, short blonde hair, and breasts that, while not huge, still demand attention. Expensive running shoes. Maybe a young lawyer. A kept wife. The schoolteacher-daughter of some captain of industry.

In any case, my first customer.

"Are you him?" she asks.

"I hope so," I reply, making a mental note to thank my mother for getting me out of the house in something other than jeans and a T-shirt.

"You don't look like a drug dealer."

"Who said I was a drug dealer?" Never admit you're a dealer, Rico had warned me. You let them establish intent to sell, and you might as well be handing them the keys to your cell.

She sighs. "No, no, yes, no, yes."

"What's that?"

"The answers to the questions you're about to ask me."

"You've done this before."

"Yes," she says, bouncing impatiently on her toes. "Have you?"

"Can you tell it's my first day on the job?"

"Congratulations. Can we get this over with? I'm expected home."

She pulls the money out of her shoe. I hand her the bag. She slides it into the back of her pants and jogs away. So much for meeting new friends on the job.

MY NEXT MEETING IS ON Wall Street, a straight shot downtown on the 2. Joseph slithers past me on the train between Chambers and Fulton, slipping a bag into my jacket. I emerge from the station into a light rain with ten minutes to spare. Taking shelter in a doorway, I watch the thousand-dollar suits, water beading and rolling off their gelled hair as they yammer into portable telephones. I root for lightning.

Ten minutes past the appointed meeting time, I notice a kid my age who could have been me. A much douchier version of me. His hair is slicked back like the rest of the Yuppies, but his suit gives him away: It's an off-the-rack version of the standard uniform. He tries to make eye contact with me, so I give him a half-nod.

"Hey," he says. "You looking for Danny?"

"That depends," I ask. "Are you Danny?"

"Maybe. Why?"

"Because then I'd know that I wasn't looking for you," I say. "Guy I'm meeting's supposed to be wearing Armani."

"Take it easy, *Dockers*," he says, insulting the pants my mother bought for me. Now I really don't like this guy. "Danny's in his office. He told me to come find you."

I angle myself toward the subway, ready to run—another one of Rico's suggestions. "The proxy is like a red alert," he told me, surprising me with his use of the word "proxy." "Nobody is so lazy that he ain't gonna pick up his own shit, you know what I mean?" On the other hand, the police, in Rico's experience, were more than capable of "these kinds of subterfuges."

I tell him that I don't know any Dannys.

"Danny Carr," he insists. "He said there's a Benjamin in it for you if you come up to his office."

Oddly enough, the offer of extra money is actually a positive sign that this *isn't* a setup. Another Rico-ism: The police can't make a case against someone they bribe into committing a crime. "Why would I want to come up to his office?"

He holds out his palms and shrugs. "Working for Danny means doing what he asks you to do when he asks you to do it. Or as Danny says, *why* is not a component of my job."

"My heart bleeds for you. But I don't work for Danny."

"Neither will I if you don't follow me back up there. Come on. A hundred bucks for, like, ten extra minutes of work."

I look for any other suspicious signs. Like I'd know. "Are you a cop?" I ask per the standard script.

"Fuck no." He smiles nervously. "Why would you think I'm a cop?"

My spirit of caution finally gives way to the greedy desire to more than double my daily pay. I follow the kid across the street into an office building. We walk past a front desk, nodding at the security guard, and ride an empty elevator to the twenty-third floor.

As soon as the doors close, he extends a hand. "Rick Cleary."

"Okay." I ignore his hand.

"So are you, like, Danny's drug dealer?"

"I really don't know what you're talking about."

"I know, I know. Just the question about me being a cop." I scan the elevator for potential hidden cameras, pretending not to hear him. "You don't want to talk about it, that's chill."

We reach the twenty-third floor, where a reception desk welcomes us to DC Investments. The desk is empty, as are most of the cubicles Rick leads me past on the way to the corner office. Inside, a guy in the right suit but with Art Garfunkel hair barks what sounds like Japanese into a speakerphone. Danny Carr, I presume. Noticing me, he gestures toward the couch. Noticing Rick, he waves angrily toward the exit. Rick backs out like a geisha, closing the door behind him.

As I settle into the black leather, Danny reaches into a cabinet behind him, pulling out an unfamiliar appliance that reminds me of a birdhouse I built in tenth-grade wood shop. This birdhouse is wired for electricity, I note when he jams the plug into the wall, causing a light in the box to glow neon green. Without breaking from his conversation in Japanese, Danny returns to the cabinet for a two-foot length of surgical tubing and a small metal disk about the size of a can of Skoal.

"Where's Carlos?" he says, finishing his call.

Carlos was my predecessor, the kid I'd seen smashing his Motorola in the stairwell. "I'm the new Carlos," I say.

"New Carlos." He chuckles. "Like New Coke. Let's hope you last a little longer. You don't look like a drug dealer."

"It's funny. Everyone keeps telling me that."

"Carlos and I had a few arrangements, is all. Among them a little extra juice for making the trip upstairs." He peels two hundred-dollar bills from a money clip and hands them to me. "You don't mind, do you?"

"I guess not." My eyes drift back toward the birdhouse.

"It's called a vaporizer," he explains. "My cousin sent me one from Los *On-hell-eez*. It's like a health food thing. No tar—just pure THC. Just takes forever to heat up." Danny pulls out a pack of Vantages and bangs it against his hand a couple of times before offering me one. I shake my head no. My pager's already buzzing again.

"I should get going."

"The Candyman's work is never done. But while I've got you here, let me run something else by you. Another arrangement I had with Carlos. These skimpy-ass quarters are fine for the office," he says, gesturing at the bag I've placed on his desk. "But for the weekend, I need a little weight. I know: They've already told you they don't do weight."

He's right: Rico made it clear, during our time together, that transactions involving anything above and beyond the "gentleman's quarter" are forbidden by papal decree. It's the kind of modesty that keeps the Pontiff under the radar and out of jail. It's also, he hinted, the reason why Carlos was fired.

"First day," I say, holding up my hands in surrender.

"Sure," Danny says, handing me a business card. "When you change your mind, there's an extra five hundred dollars a week in it for you."

•

I MEET THE NEXT CUSTOMER at the corner of Twenty-third
Street and Seventh Avenue. My first thought is: *Who knew so
many beautiful women smoked pot?*

My next thought: *She's a he.* Not a transvestite . . . just, I
have to admit, a very attractive man wearing skintight leather
pants and black mascara.

He screams when he sees me. "Yah! Pleeeease tell me
you've got the damn weed!" He stomps his foot impatiently
while I take him through the standard script, but manages all
the right answers. Until we get to the part about the money.

"Fuuuuck!" He fumbles through his pockets, coming up
with a condom and some lint.

"We're done here," I say, walking back toward the subway
station.

He grabs my shoulder. I spin toward him, putting on what
I hope is a scowl. I consider myself more lover than fighter,
but I'm not about to get intimidated by a guy wearing eye-
liner. "You're violating my personal space," I say.

"Follow me back to the crib. Kristof's got the scratch."

"Call again when you're flush." I turn again to leave.

"It's right down the goddamn street. You know the Hotel
Chelsea?"

5

I HAVE SEEN *SID AND NANCY* FOURTEEN TIMES.
Despite what you probably think, I'm not some
crazy-ass obsessive fan. I mean, it's a great movie,
even if they got Johnny Rotten all wrong. A love story that
isn't full of shit, that recognizes the stupidity of it all—true
love, impossible in the real world, only leads to pain.

But that's not the reason I've seen it fourteen times. I've
seen it fourteen times because it was the only movie Daphne
owned, and we were usually too lazy, wasted, or horny to
make it to the video store.

"Remind you of anyone we know?" she'd ask me each time
after it ended. A question that should have been, let's face it, a
gigantic red flag, given that—sorry if I'm spoiling the ending
for you—Sid winds up stabbing Nancy to death in a room at
the Chelsea Hotel.

But then Daphne would sing Leonard Cohen: "I remember—

you well in the Chelsea Hotel, you were talking so brave and so sweet, giving me head on the unmade bed . . ."

At which point she would stop singing and reenact the scene—the TV was conveniently located in the bedroom. Thankfully, unlike the song or the movie, Daphne's version always had a happy ending.

We used to talk about staying at the Chelsea for what I assumed would be a night of mind-blowing sex. Before she tried to kill me. Still, I kind of owe it to myself to see the place.

"In and out," I say to Leatherpants. "And that's not like, you know, a metaphor for anything. I'm serious. You better not offer to blow me when we get there."

He's already racing down the street. "You know, for a drug dealer," he yells over his shoulder, "you're dressed like a real asshole."

The hotel, a hundred years old, looks her age. Not so much from the outside, but inside there's an ongoing war between patchwork and decay. The smart money is on decay. But I still feel a tingle when I see the familiar lobby, nearly every square inch of wall space burnished by paintings whose placement and artistic value both seemed to have been chosen completely at random.

I follow Leatherpants—who by now has introduced himself as Nate—past the front desk toward the elevators. A guy in an expensive sweater, possibly cashmere, pressed slacks, and tassel loafers looks up from the floor he's mopping. He examines us through a pair of glasses hanging from a cord around his neck. He doesn't look pleased.

"Hello, Herman!" says Nate, waving as he shoots past the guy onto the square-spiral case, ripping off three steps at a time. I jog after him, feeling Herman's stare on my back. We don't stop until we reach the fourth floor.

I'm not sure what I expected. Kind of a punk-rock *Animal House*, maybe. The peeling wallpaper and rusting pipes feel right, but the hallway is quiet and empty. It occurs to me that for the second time in my first three Meet-Ups, I'm violating the rule against following customers back to their rooms. The police could be waiting for me. Or worse, I'm going to get jumped and rolled when I step through the door.

Nate bounds down the hallway like a manic jackalope, planting his feet in front of Room 411.

"Janis Joplin," he says.

"I'm sorry?"

"This was Janis's suite."

Then he opens the door, sucking all of the fear and disappointment out of the air.

It's backstage at a rock concert born in the imagination of a horny teenage boy: beer cans, bottles of Jack half-drunk, rock nymphettes half-clothed. Guns N' Roses blasting from a box radio on the kitchenette's counter. A topless blonde sways to the music on top of the guy she's got pinned to the couch, hypnotizing him with tits too perfect to be real. A Eurotrash dude with a clove cigarette and a brown jacket that might be sewn from the skins of baby deer cheers on two brunettes in stretchy miniskirts, asses so sculpted they should be in a museum, as they face off in a dance that makes the *Lambada* look like the Virginia Reel. The part of my brain that isn't gaping like a tourist wonders why I can't see any panty lines.

"Is that you?" comes a voice from an attached bedroom. I turn toward it in time to see a perfect female silhouette framed in the doorway against the sunlight, a trucker's mud flap come to life. Then she steps into the room, and there's nothing left to remind me of a trucker. Her eyelids seem to open a fraction of an inch higher than they should, leaving extra space for her eyes—radioactive blue, lively and intelligent. High cheekbones softened by pillowy lips and auburn hair that cascades in waves down to the small of her back. A body whose long legs and curves would have been a genius plastic surgeon's signature work had they not been entirely the real thing. She's wearing a concert tee with three-quarter sleeves, white panties, and nothing else. She looks at me quizzically. "You're not Nate."

Nate's across the room with the Euro-dude, who's reaching for his wallet. "No," I reply, scrambling for an opening line. But I'm too slow.

"Well then close the damn door," she says. By the time I step inside and close the door behind me, Nate is greeting her with a kiss.

"There's my angel," he says, twirling her around like a dancer. "I was just securing your degeneracy of choice." He pulls her close, slips a $100 bill into the band of her panties, and spins her into me. We realize at the same time—and with roughly equal levels of embarrassment—that I'm expected to remove the cash from her intimates. We attend to the transaction with a minimum of eye contact.

"At least my degeneracy is all-natural," she says. I remove the bag of weed from my pocket and hand it to her.

"Now come on, sugar," Nate says, raising an eyebrow toward the couch. "Artificial has its charms. Wouldn't you say so, Clem?" The guy on the couch seems to agree, his reply muffled by the blonde's bodacious endowments.

"You're a pig," says the silhouette, returning with the weed to whatever magical lair she emerged from. Nate grins and follows, stopping only to punch me on the shoulder.

"You're the man," he tells me. "Stay and party. I'll bet Kristof will share."

Across the room, the two brunettes—Kristof's apparent bounty—interlock their tongues in a passionate kiss. I look down at my pager. It is barely eleven o'clock in the morning.

"I've got to get back to work."

"Well, come on by after," he says, closing the bedroom door behind him. "The party never ends."

Six hours later, having ditched my sports jacket on a nearby fire escape, I walk back into the Chelsea. The man in the maybe-cashmere sweater sits behind the front desk, clearly in his natural element. He is the master of this environment. Whether by optical illusion or some other arrangement, the light in the room actually seems to bend toward him.

I smile, wave as I'd seen Nate do, say "Hello, Herman!" and make for the stairs.

"I don't baleeve we've met," Herman says. His voice is what you might call "New York Authentic," nasal and low-pitched, and amplifies his already potent dominion over the lobby. "Yuh wuh heah earliah, wit' Nate."

"I was just headed back upstairs to see him," I reply. But my feet have stopped moving and the staircase—another optical illusion—seems to be moving farther away from me.

"No yuh not. Not unless yuh been vetted wit' me fihst."

"I didn't realize this was that kind of joint," I reply, a lame attempt at vaudeville humor. Something about the accent. "You want to see my calling card?"

"Huh," he snorts. "Yuh tink I don't know yuh a drug dealah?"

Ouch. I cycle through my brain for a response until a bell goes off. It's the elevator. We both turn toward the opening doors. The silhouette is slightly different, but I know immediately it's the same girl.

She steps into the lobby. Her wavy hair is slicked back, still wet from a shower. She's wearing a Catholic schoolgirl miniskirt, 18-eye Doc Martens, and an oversized leather jacket that probably belongs to Nate.

"Hi," I say, a little too eagerly.

"Hi," she replies, politely concealing her inability to place me. Her radioactive blues are stony red.

"When I was here earlier. This morning. Nate told me to stop by the party later."

"The party ended hours ago." Herman looks down when she says this, apparently deeply saddened by the news.

"I'm an idiot," I suggest.

She looks me over. Now I'm wishing I were wearing something other than wool slacks and a button-down. "Probably," she finally says. "But you're coherent enough to have a drink with me, aren't you?"

"Sure," I say. "I pride myself on my coherence."

Herman slinks back into the shadows behind the desk. I follow her down a corridor that connects the lobby to the Mexican restaurant next door, where mariachi music pipes in through tinny speakers and the waiters are dressed for a bull-fight. We slide into a booth and order margaritas and cheese nachos.

Her name is K. Actually, it's Katherine, but she adopted the initial because she thought it would help her get started as a professional model. Her first job took her from her native Northern California—"Sunnyvale!" she chirps with an exaggeratedly fake smile—across the Pacific Ocean, where she spent three months doing catalog shoots in South Korea, Japan, and Hong Kong. "Amazing," she says, "but incredibly lonely." She met Nate during a return trip to San Francisco—he and Clem, the guy I'd seen getting dry-humped on the couch, formed half of an L.A. glam-rock revival band called Venomous Iris. A drunken hookup at a bar segued into a drunken weekend in Napa Valley and an invitation from Nate to follow him back to L.A., where he was scheduled to play a few dates on the Sunset Strip. He was tall and sexy and spoke English and what the fuck, following a band for a while would probably be fun. Clem told her from the start that Nate was a guitar god, and he hadn't been lying: The band got signed to a deal and their first album, *Love Vampire,* won over a few influential reviewers who dug the fusion between GN'R and Bowie. Sales weren't amazing, but they were promising enough to earn them a shot at a second album. Only the scene in L.A. was . . . you know, *L.A.*—not exactly conducive to getting shit done. They somehow hooked up with Kristof, who'd spent some time working for the record companies and also possibly as an international arms dealer, but we don't talk about that, who offered to not only manage the band but bankroll a trip to New York City, because no distractions in New York, right? That last part was sarcasm, K. assures me.

They moved into the Chelsea eight months ago. Herman was thrilled to have them as guests, giving them the suite that had belonged to Janis because, as he told them, he truly believed in Nate's *ahtistic pahtental.* Herman loves artists, K. explains. She thinks the paintings in the lobby are gifts he's accepted over the years in lieu of rent.

We order a second round of margaritas. "How's the album coming?" I ask.

"Ah," she says with a sigh. "The album."

One month into their stay at the Chelsea, Brett, the bass player, died of a brain aneurysm.

The grieving process went on for nearly two months before they met Brett's replacement, Ralphie from Queens, during Thrash Day at CBGB. Ralphie was good, probably better than Brett—very Les Claypool—but Brett was like mellow peace-sign dude, while Ralphie is, you know, *intense.*

The retooled Venomous Iris managed to record four songs before Ralphie punched Clem in the face, which, spend any time with Clem, is pretty much inevitable. Ralphie took off and the next three guys sucked. Scott, the drummer, got so fed up with the scene he quit and enrolled at Columbia—grad school in psychology. But Clem finally patched things up with Ralphie and they were going to start recording again as soon as Scott was done with finals. Nate thought the album—now they were calling it *Hell's Sweet Gravity*—might be done by Christmas, but with all of the holiday parties, postparties, and postparty recovery time, it would be a major accomplishment not to mention a minor miracle if they were done by spring.

K. looks at me to gauge my interest. "Am I boring you yet?" she asks. I tell her she's not and order another round of drinks to prove it.

In another bit of irony, what had been bad for the band had been good for K. A week into their stay, on the elevator—the Chelsea's elevator is *quite* the scene—she met Ray Mondavi. He lived on the eighth floor, where he had a photography studio, and he offered to take a new set of modeling photos to help get her back into circulation. That wasn't *all* he offered, but if you know Ray you know he just can't help himself and no, nothing ever happened. He showed the pictures to John at Elite who booked her an ad on a billboard that had brought traffic on Broadway to a near halt and now John was claiming that she was at the top of the list for next year's *Sports Illustrated* swimsuit issue. Not that she believes him—she knows all the stories—but shit, fingers crossed, right?

K. crosses her fingers, waving them at me like she's casting a spell. "I am now officially finished with talking about me," she says. "You're up."

Three margaritas are exactly enough to get me started on Daphne. "We'll save my story for our next date," I say, placing two twenties on the table to cover the tab.

"I'm not sure Nate would like that." When she grins, I think of that movie with the cartoon rabbit. *I'm not bad. I'm just drawn that way.* I can see why K. would make an effective fashion model.

I rise to my feet to leave. Always leave them wanting more. But it doesn't take me too long to recognize the flaw in my strategy: I have nowhere to go.

"You're going home?" she asks, not quite innocently.

"Yeah, no, I don't really have a home. . . ."

"Oh . . ."

I can almost hear the doors closing in her brain as her opinion of me moves from "cute mystery guy" to "sad homeless waif."

"I mean I'm staying in Long Island until I find a place in the city," I add quickly. "I just started looking."

"There's always the Chelsea," she says cheerily.

When a door closes, I reflect, *a window opens.* My second idiotic platitude in thirty seconds, I realize, a sure sign that I'm getting drunk. "I don't know. I got the distinct impression from Herman that he might not like me hanging around."

"I'll bet I can change his mind." The stony lethargy has drained from her eyes, replaced by something competitive and maybe a little feral. I let her drag me back to the front desk, where for Herman's benefit I am reinvented as a struggling poet who's just inherited a small sum from a dear aunt whose dying request was that I use it to launch my career. I have a unique and important voice, a cross between Stevens and Bukowski, and the *New Yorker* recently expressed interest.

I can tell that Herman's not an idiot, but K. isn't the kind of woman you're inclined to argue with, not if you're inclined toward women. In the end, her radioactive blues trump his skeptical stare and I am offered Room 242, at a rent there's no way I can afford, just as soon as I can come up with first and last plus a $1,200 deposit. "I nuh ha diffacut poetry can be," he assures me.

I shake Herman's hand, give K. an awkward cross between a hug and a kiss, and exit the lobby into the icy night. My jacket is still hanging right where I left it. I reach inside and find Danny Carr's business card.

6

THE LIMO—MORE OF A TOWN CAR, REALLY— pulls up to the corner. The window rolls down. Danny's got a shit-eating grin.

"Get in," he says.

I walk around to the other side of the car and climb inside. As I close the door behind me, I realize Danny's grin doesn't have anything to do with eating shit. There is a head, female by the looks of it, bobbing between his legs.

"Jesus," I manage.

"You don't mind, do you, buddy?"

"Uh, no. I guess I don't."

"I was glad that you called. You've reconsidered."

"Not yet," I say. Better not to sound too desperate. "Just considering my options."

"I'm not giving you an option. Options are like, rare or medium rare. Onions, no onions. Brunette or redhead. Which are you, by the way?" He taps the bobbing head. She disengages from Danny's crotch with a wet sound that makes me feel ickier than I already do.

"It's red, asshole," she says.

"We'll see about that," he replies, guiding her head back between his legs. "What I'm offering you, buddy, isn't an option. It's an opportunity. An opportunity to double your weekly salary." He gestures toward a row of bottles on a built-in shelf. "Fix yourself a drink while I talk." I pour a whiskey named after a Scottish glen I've never heard of. The taste makes me think I've never really had scotch before, that up until now I've been drinking piss water.

"Like I said at the office, the quarters, or what you guys pass off as quarters, they're fine for the week. But on the weekend, I entertain. Place in Bridgehampton, another in Miami. You'll see for yourself. But then, there, I need pounds."

"I've got to be honest with you. I think you've got me mistaken for someone who has some juice. I just deliver the stuff."

"I'm not asking you to grow it for me."

"No, I mean, I don't control the flow. They give me one bag, one customer."

"You ever heard of the expression 'thinking outside the box'?"

My gaze is drawn involuntarily back toward the bobbing head. "Uh, no."

"Business school bullshit. But it's actually a useful idea.

Don't let your perceptions of your circumstances limit your possibilities."

"I don't have any idea what you're talking about."

"If the only way to secure more product is to sell to more customers, then sell to more customers."

"Aha," I say. "You mean you could call in more than once a day."

"Me? No. Too busy. But you could." The car pulls to a stop. "Take five," he says to the head. "We're at the hotel." I smile at her as she smooths off her dress, both because she's lovely and because I don't want to catch a wayward glimpse of Danny's exposed package.

"This is where we get out," Danny says as a valet opens the door. The lady exits the car. "Where do you need to go?"

"The train," I reply. "Grand Central."

"No, I mean, where do you need to go?"

"Levittown?"

"Mel!" he says to the driver. "Take this man to Levittown."

"Yes, sir," the driver responds.

Danny hands me ten hundred-dollar bills. "Get me five extra bags before this weekend. The rest is yours to keep." He jumps out of the cab. "I know I can count on you, buddy!"

The car pulls away from the hotel. I settle back into the seat, careful to avoid any residue Danny and his "date" may have left behind. There's a copy of the *New York Post* stuck in the back of the seat. A kid in the Bronx, seventeen, shot dead during a high school argument. Two cops, accused of kicking and beating a protester in Tompkins Square Park, found in-

nocent and acquitted of all charges. A composite sketch that
could have been any black man with a mustache, this one in
particular wanted for breaking up a subway mugging, as he'd
stabbed one of the muggers to death in the process. The stories reinforce Uncle Marvin's view of New York City, a fucked-
up place to be sure. But they don't describe the city I'm seeing
from the back of the limo. I feel like a king in a carriage, the
rain and the lights and the constant motion all a private performance for my benefit.

One hour and three Glen-whatevers later, the car pulls
up in front of my parents' three-bed, two-bath Cape Cod,
one of dozens like it mass-produced after World War II. I
slink quietly up to my room and remove the cash from my
pocket. I jam it into a wooden box, some ornate thing an ex-
girlfriend brought me back from India, that I keep on my
dresser.

"That's a lot of scratch," says my father.

He's sitting on my bed, suit rumpled as the sheets, his eyes
a shade of light red I recognize as the short sabbatical between the night's second and third scotch. In other words, he's
keeping roughly the same pace as me. "They keeping you late
at the office?" he asks.

"Grabbed a beer with a friend of mine."

"Your friend's got a nice car."

"Belongs to the company. I had to work late. Is there a
reason why you're in my room?"

"Your room." He pounds his chest. "My house."

"Whatever." I flip on the TV. "I'll be out of here soon."

"You lied, you know. To your mother."

"About what?"

"About your job," he says, nodding at the box on the dresser. "Or do temp agencies pay in cash?"

I'm about to make up an excuse, who knows what, when he continues. "I'm not going to say anything. Don't worry. But you'd be doing your old man a solid if you spotted him a hundred bucks."

"You want to borrow a hundred dollars from me?"

"You mind, kid? I'm a little stuck this month."

"Stuck?"

"You know what I mean."

I do, in fact, know what he means. Even I've noticed Dad's recent attention to his appearance. More frequent haircuts. More fashionable shoes. Mysterious tubes of Binaca breath spray springing up around the house. I've also seen Mom paying extra attention to the bank and credit card statements, putting a serious crimp in Dad's ability to finance an extramarital affair. My guess is that the hundred-dollar "loan" would pay for lunch *pour deux* at Beefsteak Charlie's, with enough left over for an hour at the conveniently close-but-not-too-close Starlight Inn.

"Sure, Dad," I say. "You've done so much for me."

I retrieve a bill from the box and hand it to him. He rises to his feet and claps me on the shoulder. "That's my boy. So where is it?"

"Where's what?"

"The restaurant where you're working."

I almost cry out with relief—he knows exactly nothing. "Must not be too shabby," he adds, stumbling off toward *his* third scotch of the night. "Like I said, that's a lot of scratch."

7

IF YOU'RE ANYTHING LIKE ME, THE IDEA OF being surrounded by supermodels might be something you've dreamed about. If you're the kind of person who likes your dreams intact—i.e., free of puncture holes—you probably don't want to read what's next: The experience is overrated.

I'm not saying the models are overrated. Anything but. You might wonder if up close they're just regular gals with decent bone structure and expert hair and makeup artists. They aren't. They're perfect, or close enough.

And it's not that they're stupid, or insecure, or vain, even though some of them are. Maybe most of them. But beauty forgives intellectual shortcomings.

No, what's overrated is the experience of meeting a supermodel. Because deep down, you're hoping that you and she will fall in love. Or lust. Or just find something to talk about for more than thirty seconds. But you won't. Supermodels are like professional athletes or violin prodigies: brilliant but limited in worldview. Maybe you're the kind of guy who knows a lot about strappy shoes or applying foundation. But if you're dreaming about bedding supermodels, you're probably not that guy.

You tell yourself that you can overlook this lack of connection. And you're right. You can. But *she* can't. Women are all about connection. Or connections. And unless you can bring at least one of those to the table, you might as well be speaking Martian.

At least that's been my experience tonight. Every conversation has petered out once it's been established that I'm not famous, I don't work for an agency, and I don't know anything about strappy shoes.

I can't say the same for my wingman, Ray. He is a black belt in the art of the flirtatious insult, which seems to be exactly the right jujitsu to snare these lovelies. As in three telephone numbers so far. His real talent lies in his ability to identify the microscopic flaw, invisible to most, which causes the poor supermodel to spend anguished hours in front of the mirror. The spot where a wrinkle will one day appear. A millimeter of sag in the ass. A calf muscle slightly out of proportion to the thigh.

"I can't believe they let you go out in that," I hear him tell a seemingly flawless specimen. A few minutes later, she's writing her phone number on his hand.

He rubs the ink off as soon as she leaves. "The game gets

old, doesn't it?" He yawns, holding up three fingers. "Three yawns. I only give a place ten. Nothing good ever happens after ten yawns."

I met Ray the day I moved into the Chelsea, when he introduced himself to Tana.

Even with the extra cash from my arrangement with Danny Carr, it still takes me three weeks to save enough for the room. Tana, home again after taking her winter finals, offers to help me move. Which turns out to be code for bitching about her latest problems with Glenn and gifting me with a tiny cactus from the Duane Reade around the corner. It's on me to wrestle my overstuffed duffel bag (everything worthwhile from my closet) and milk crate (an IBM Selectric II and a few books from Freshman Lit I hoped might sell me as a poet) up the stairs and down the narrow hallway to Room 242.

Somewhere along the way two things happen: Tana turns into a man with a rapid-fire Southern accent that effectively ends any Yankee stereotypes about *drawls*; and my bag gets wedged in the hallway, rendering me unable to move. I tug with a level of force that's quickly becoming embarrassing. I wonder which is going to break first, the strap or my shoulder. Then, suddenly, the weight of the duffel is gone.

I slide out from underneath the bag. My savior turns out to be a muscled gym rat with a long black ponytail and a wispy attempt at a goatee. He strikes a pose like Atlas, my bag as his globe, and extends his free hand. "Ray Mondavi," he says.

He's the same Ray Mondavi who took K's photos and jump-started her career. The Southern accent is a residue from his native Richmond, Virginia, the express-train delivery a by-product of the five years he'd spent in Miami, lugging equipment for a fashion photographer whose name Tana recognizes. While I hang my wardrobe from an exposed pipe—Room 242 turns out to be sans closet (or bathroom)—Ray keeps Tana in stitches with a "models are as dumb as you think they are" story from a recent shoot in Turks and Caicos. His eyes drill into hers except when he's checking out her body, seeming not so much sleazy as professionally detached, like a tailor eyeing a guy for a suit. He breaks concentration from his internal calculus only twice: the first time to look at me to let me know that he knows that I know he's checking her out, the second to see if it's bothering me. I give Ray my blessing with the slightest of nods. Despite our reputation for insensitivity and emotional retardation, we men have a surprisingly rich nonverbal vocabulary. Especially when there's a lady present.

"You should let me take your picture," Ray tells Tana.

"Yeah, right," she says, giggling.

"I'm serious. Not for the runway—you don't have the stilts for that—but print. . . . You're a classic Ellen von Unwerth girl. Sensual, like Claudia or Carré."

Tana is blushing. "I'll think about it," she says.

"I hope you will," Ray replies, backing out of the room. "Welcome to the Chelsea."

I'm grateful to see him leave, not because I don't like listening to his game—it's already clear that this man might be able to teach my inner dog a few tricks—but because the room isn't big enough for three people. The double bed takes up most of the space; the sink beneath a cracked mirror accounts for the rest—anything requiring more elaborate plumbing will have to take place in the communal bathroom down the hall. I'd hoped for a balcony, like in *Sid and Nancy*, but will have to settle for a fire escape with a view of the neighboring brick wall.

"At least you've got a patio," Tana says as she climbs back inside through the window, having placed the cactus in a cold, sunless corner where a week later it will die. She sits on the edge of the bed, testing its bounce. "So when are you going to break this bad boy in?" she asks.

This turns out to be an Excellent Question.

During my first week at the Chelsea, I'm a ghost, invisible to the other residents, whom I glimpse occasionally behind closing doors. I walk by Nate and K.'s suite often enough to seem like a stalker, and a few more times after that. I press my ear against the door, failing each time to hear any hint of the promised nonstop party.

A coy smile from an Amazonian stunner in the fabled elevator briefly arouses my hopes. Until "she" responds to my overeager introduction: Mika has a voice three octaves lower than mine and, by my best guess, a functioning penis. The only predictable human interaction comes from Herman, a more or less permanent presence at the front desk, who asks after my poetry every time he sees me. Given his skills as a bullshit detector, I do my best to keep these conversations short.

For the first time in forever, I am lonely. I ring Tana almost every night from the pay phone in the Mexican restaurant. She welcomes my calls, having finally broken things off with Glenn, but the steady background marimba and the charges exacted by New York Telephone keep us from rambling. I even call my mother once, but her maternal curiosity about my job forces me into increasingly elaborate lies, and her questions about my social life leave me even more depressed.

In a couple of weeks I might have enough saved up for a social life. But for now it's hot dogs and slices and nights spent alone. The drafty old hotel turns out to have a tough time holding on to heat, with the notable exception of my miniature room and its exposed hot-water plumbing. Nighttime temperatures often reach the nineties. I learn to use my window like a tub faucet in reverse, replenishing the room as needed with below-freezing air. It gives me something to do while I lie awake at night trying to remember why I thought living in this place would be better than home.

During the day, I mine my interactions with the customers for whatever fleeting nuggets of warmth I can find. The Upper East Side jogger gives up her name ("Liz") after I compliment her eyes, then tears off like a woman with more important things to do. Charlie, a kid about my age who works nights sweeping up an underground card game, is usually good for fifteen minutes of conversation before he dozes off into stoned slumber on whichever park bench in Union Square promises the most sun.

And Danny Carr.

Most people smoke pot to mellow out. Danny is not one of those people. The man is what my parents might call a "dynamo," and the weed only stokes those fires. I'm more inclined to use the word "asshole," but he's more than doubling my take-home pay each week for the equivalent of a few prank phone calls, so I go along to get along.

Each workday I make two calls to the Pontiff's toll-free customer line. At first, I use a different accent each time: Park Avenue, Puerto Rico, Staten Island, and one that starts Haitian but rapidly deteriorates into *Diff'rent Strokes*: "Whatchoo talkin' 'bout, Mister D.?" Luckily, Billy's years of taking calls from the highly stoned means that it's pretty much impossible to sound too weird. But I'm no Rich Little: Impersonations have never been my thing. I max out at six, maybe seven voices that sound remotely convincing. So I transform them into regular customers, requiring the purchase of a small black notebook at Duane Reade to keep track of my polyethnic cast of characters and their imaginary smoking habits. I don't want to fuck up. While I'm not exactly scamming the Pontiff—if anything, I'm generating more business—delivering two pounds to Danny each week certainly exposes me to risks outside the operation's comfort zone, something Rico, during my audition, impressed upon me *never* to do.

Friday night, my third week of moonlighting for Danny, I return to my room at the hotel after making my last legitimate delivery. I load my shirt with the bags. "That's quite a potbelly," I say to the cracked mirror. I open the door before the mirror can reply, jogging down the stairs toward the subway and Danny's office. Only this time I nearly steamroll K. as she's walking into the elevator.

"Hey, you," she says. She's freshly showered, hasn't bothered with makeup, and isn't suffering for it in the slightest. My heart's beating like a jackhammer, but I've never been more lucid. I finally have an honest answer to the question of why I chose to live at the Chelsea.

"I've been looking for you," I say. "About that second date."

She smiles. "It's going to have to be a quickie. I've got to get back to Nate. They're flying to Chicago tonight and they'll never make it to the airport without me."

"I can work fast when I have to."

"A fast worker, huh?"

"Don't get me wrong. I prefer to take my time."

"You know, I'm not that easy."

"Me neither," I fire back. "But I'm open to rehabilitation."

She smiles again. Could my rap actually be working? Her eyes dart back and forth, signaling an internal debate. "I've got a show tomorrow night," she finally says. "Versace."

"Congratulations."

"Thank you, thank you," she says with a curtsy. "But would you believe that I still get nervous up there? Lame, I know, but I could really use a rooting section and with Nate out of town . . ."

"I'm there!" I say, grinning a little too much.

"Don't get any ideas: I'm a good girl. But I can't say the same for all of my friends. A roomful of beautiful, insecure women of questionable character. A guy like you might do all right."

"'A guy like me'? I believe I've just been insulted."

She gently slaps my cheek. "Poor baby. There'll be a pass for you at the door, if you can get over the hurt. Ray's going too. Maybe you guys can share a cab." She struts past me into the elevator. She's smiling as the doors close shut.

"You shud write a pome abut hah," Herman chimes in, having caught the scene from his perch behind the desk.

"I just might," I reply, scurrying out into the street to avoid further interrogation. I let my momentum carry me to Seventh Avenue, where I catch the train downtown.

DESPITE K.'S SUGGESTION, WE DON'T need a cab—it's only a ten-block walk to the show, a former slaughterhouse in the Meatpacking District that's been reclaimed as an "art space." Like a true Dixie gentleman, Ray brings along a flask of Southern Comfort to warm us along the way, leaving us nicely lacquered by the time we take our seats. We hoot and holler when K. struts out for the first time, decked in a fluorescent green smock I couldn't imagine ever seeing on a civilian. Like the true professional she is, she ignores us completely.

A half hour later—about twenty-five minutes after the

novelty of seeing so many imperious beauties march in, spin, and march out again has run its course—I wake to the sound of applause. The fashion designer rides a supermodel stampede to the stage.

"Lucky dude," I say.

"Tell that to his boyfriend," Ray replies. "Now let's have some fun."

Which is when I begin striking out, and Ray starts yawning. He's all the way up to seven before K. appears, having completed her circuit of the industry types Ray calls Big Swinging Dicks: "Especially the women!" She's still made up but dressed for downtown, having shed the Day-Glo smock in favor of a one-piece black velvet minidress and her 18-eye Docs.

"Yow!" Ray howls at her, pulling his hand back as if he's been scorched. "You owned it, lady!" K. accepts the compliment with a curtsy and a smile. "But I don't know what they were thinking putting you in that rig with the Mork from Ork suspenders," he continues. "You need tits for that one."

"You're an asshole," K. says, but she's laughing. She looks to me for my reaction, which right now is to smile like a moron. When I fail to reply within a socially acceptable time frame, she throws me a lifeline. "A few of us are headed down to the Western."

"The Western Diner," Ray says. "Most ironically named restaurant in the world."

It doesn't take long to figure out what he means. I'd noticed the Western Diner during my transactions with Union

Square Charlie and, having seen the place only in daylight, been fooled by the name. Nobody's dining; in fact, most of the patrons—models, club kids, and a smattering of minor celebrities with rapidly swiveling heads—are poster children for eating disorders. We skip through the velvet ropes, our entrance blazed by K. and two femmes with the faces of angels but names too important to share with me, landing us in a coveted corner booth. The ladies order something called mojitos and excuse themselves to go to the bathroom. "Riding the rails," Ray says as they leave. "At least they'll be horny. Which one do you want?"

"I guess K.'s out of bounds," I venture.

"Waste of time. Nate doesn't deserve her, but he's got the whole rock star thing working for him." Ray wiggles his fingers in the air. "Chick voodoo. He's got his teeth in her like fucking Dracula."

"I must have missed the fang marks."

"They're everywhere. Blood, heart, soul, and pussy. Whatever it is you want, you ain't getting it from her."

"In that case," I suggest, "I'll let you choose first."

Ray shrugs. "I don't even like white women. I need a little T'ang in my 'tang," he says, stretching his eyes into slants to make his point. "But I don't like going to bed hungry, either. Let's just lay 'em as they play."

Twenty minutes later, I'm locked into conversation with one of K.'s friends, a brunette who finally introduces herself as Stella. She's locked into whatever's going on behind me. After a few more swings and misses, I scan the crowd for Ray. He's

on the dance floor, taking advantage of the current disco revival to spin K.'s other friend around his shoulders like he's
John Travolta. Stella uses the brief distraction to slink over to
a guy I recognize from the local news.

"So," says K., returning from a buzz-maintenance session
in the bathroom. "Looks like you and Stella are hitting it off."

"A little too well. We've moved right through the passion
and the hot sex into the long, awkward silences."

"You *said* you worked fast."

"Touché," I say, lifting a glass to toast her.

"Speaking of work . . . you don't happen to be holding, do
you?"

"Oh, I see," I reply, my insult half-feigned. "I'm like your
drug Sherpa."

"It's not like that. I just need something to take the edge
off the blow. I can't stand cocaine."

"That hasn't stopped you from Hoovering the stuff," I say.
My goal is to approximate one of Ray's playful insults. What
comes out, judging by K.'s reaction, is more like a slap in the
face.

I backpedal as fast as my feet will take me. "Hell, no, lady.
I'm just trying to alienate as many people as I can tonight
with my piss-poor conversational skills. Congratulations.
You're my thousandth customer."

Her smile returns. "You're way too cute to be a drug dealer."

"I really wish you'd stop calling me that."

"Drug dealer?"

"Cute. 'Cute' is the kiss of death."

Her eyes are suddenly full of what I hope I'm reading correctly as mischief. "My kisses haven't killed anybody yet," she says, sipping her mojito through a straw.

Are we flirting? My heart seems to think so, working double time to keep the blood flowing to my brain. "I guess I'll have to take your word for it. Though to be honest, I'd like a little bit more to *go* on."

Ray sweeps back into the scene, K.'s other friend still in tow. "Tenth yawn," he says. "I've got to get this lady home before I turn into a pumpkin."

The two women exchange air kisses and K. slides the rest of the blow into the pocket of her friend's jeans. Ray pulls me close with a smooth combination of handshake and man-hug. "Yeah, boy!" he whispers—loud enough, I'm sure, for K. to hear. But she doesn't show it.

"So," she says when they're gone. "Where were we?"

"I might have been misreading the tea leaves," I reply, "but it seemed to me like we were negotiating."

"Negotiating? What were we negotiating?"

"What else? Our first kiss."

And then it happens—resting one hand against my cheek, she touches her lips to mine. Softly, gently swiping her tongue over mine. 'See?" she says. "You're still alive."

"Could be a fluke. We're going to have to try that again." This time I pull her toward me. Our lips lock, then part, tentative tongue-swipes giving way to more enthusiastic exploration. I feel a deep stirring in my loins—the Motorola.

"I think you're vibrating," she says.

I pull the pager out of my pocket and put it on the table. Tana's phone number glows from the alphanumeric display.

"Work?" asks K.

"Not tonight." I move back in for another kiss.

The table rumbles as the pager vibrates again, startling K. Then she smiles.

"Girlfriend," she says.

"Not that, either," I insist, staring at the "911" Tana's added to the display this time around. "Family. This will only take a minute."

I sprint toward the bathrooms and find an available pay phone. I hadn't bothered to equip myself with enough loose change to dial the Island, so I call collect.

"I hope somebody just died," I say after Tana's accepted the charges. "Because otherwise this is a cock block of epic proportions."

"I'm not sure," Tana says. "Your parents' house almost burned down. Is that important enough for you?"

"What?!"

"Don't worry. They're okay."

"Well, like I said, if they aren't dead. What happened? Did Dad pass out with a lit cigarette? One of his whores knock over a lantern?"

"The police think it's arson."

"Arson?" I ask, my voice somewhere between anger and disbelief. "My parents tried to burn their own house down?"

"Not your parents. Daphne. That crazy bitch tried to torch your house."

8

"ARE YOU TRYING TO FUCK MY GIRLFRIEND?"

When you're confronted with a question from a person, a legitimately crazy person with a proven penchant for violence that is, in the deepest sense of the word, *irrational*, you really only have two options: engage and hope for the best, or go numb, aka the grizzy bear defense.

I opt for the latter. But the bear keeps pawing.

"It's you," he says, "isn't it?" His severe lazy eye makes it possible that he's not addressing me at all, but a spot on the wall above and beyond my left shoulder. But I'm pretty sure he means me. I squirm in my chair and wait for Daphne to arrive.

"Leave him alone, Vincent," she says as she drifts into the room.

I'm struck by the urge to laugh: It's Daphne dressed for Halloween as a crazywoman. An inch of mousy brown hair now separates her peroxide tips from her scalp. Her eyes are glazed. She's even wearing the requisite puke green hospital gown and slide-on slippers. In a few seconds, she's going to drop the façade and smile. We'll smoke a joint and find a place to fuck.

A few seconds come and go. "I know," Daphne says. "I look like shit."

"I beg to differ," I say. "It's very punk rock." Adding, when she looks like she's about to cry, "The gown looks incredibly comfortable. You know where I can score one?"

She tries to laugh but comes up short. "I know a guy," she says. "Hey, Vincent . . . a little privacy." The bear runs anguished fingers through greasy Hitler hair and lopes off to a different area of the commons room.

Commons room. Daphne and I had one of our Top 5 Fights (Number 3, to be exact) in a room that looked a lot like this one. I'd blown off a catering gig for a party, or that's what I told Daphne. The truth was that I'd gone out to dinner with an ex-girlfriend who was passing through Ithaca on her way to Toronto. We'd begun the night talking about how weird it was that we weren't in high school anymore and ended it with her demonstrating her newfound maturity with a blow job in the front seat of her rental car. Daphne had friends at every restaurant and, once alerted, stormed directly to my dorm room. The floor's residential adviser, clearly unhappy to be woken at three A.M. by a screaming match in the hallway, threatened to call Campus Security. I dragged Daphne into the commons room, where the fight continued into daylight hours.

That was just over a year ago. It's been a long year. Today's Daphne hardly looks primed for a fight. The woman who just last week, according to the police report, splashed gasoline onto my parents' home as she screamed my name now appears to be a candidate for the world's longest nap. She's here at Kings Park, undergoing psychiatric evaluation, thanks to the Herculean efforts of Larry Kirschenbaum, whose connections and savvy kept her out of the general population at Rikers Island when my father refused to drop the charges.

"How are your parents?" she asks.

"Mom's a little ticked about her rosebushes."

"I am so sorry."

"Don't be. Insurance will cover most of it. The rest can come out of Dad's hooker fund. But hey . . . next time you want to get ahold of me?" I hold up the Motorola. "I've even got one of these now."

"Ha," she says. "What are you, a drug dealer?"

"Funny you should ask. . . ."

I fill her in on the details of my new life, minus the gloomy stretches of loneliness and my recent make-out session with a rising supermodel. Daphne manages a real smile when I tell her about the Chelsea. My words seem to nourish her and I remember why we stayed together long enough to make a list of Top 5 Fights. Sure, she's done some crazy things, but I wasn't always an honest boyfriend—if she was nuts, I'd helped to get her there. So I continue for an hour, like a rookie camper trying to make fire from flint; there are a few sparks, but in the end, Daphne's deadened eyes refuse to ignite. She rests a hand on mine, letting me know that it's okay to stop trying. I promise her I'll visit again, that she can call me anytime if she needs something, even if it's just to talk.

"There *is* one thing you can do for me," she says. "I want to find my father."

Her father left home when she was five. A few years later, he'd completely disappeared from her life. Daphne and I had a running debate over whose grass was greener, the guy with the kind of dad who steals money from his kid to take his mistress out to lunch, or the girl without a father.

"Wow," I say. "Are you sure now's a good time for that?"

"His name is Peter."

"Peter?"

"Peter Robichaux. You said if I needed anything. . . ."

"I meant something that I could actually do. Finding a guy who dropped off the map ten years ago doesn't exactly play to my strengths."

"Forget it," she says, forcing a smile. "I was just fucking with you. I'm crazy, you know."

"I'll see what I can do. Do you have any other information, an address or a phone number?"

"That's all I got," she whispers.

It's a five-minute walk to the parking lot from the building where Daphne is housed. Tana is waiting for me in her car. She holds up her wristwatch when she sees me.

"Really?" she asks.

I climb quietly into her passenger seat. I feel disoriented—spend an hour in a mental institution, and the outside world starts to seem a little weird. Tana, God bless her, parses my mood. We drive back to Levittown in silence.

9

CHRISTMAS IS HERE, IF THE CROWDS DESCEND-
ing on the Macy's in Herald Square are any indica-
tion. Which for me means that walking—the
bedrock principle of my workday—is getting tougher. Bitter
winds off the river pounce like Clouseau's man Kato, knocking about the unprepared. Mini-tsunamis form by whatever
angle of intersection causes rubber tires to launch numb-
ingly-cold waves of ash-colored snow and gravel onto already
icy sidewalks. Getting from point A to point B requires deter-
mination, concentration, and fortitude.

None of which is enough to bring me down. Then again,
I'm high.

"The whole visit to Daphne, I think it transformed me. It
just felt like I was doing the right thing. Like I had a place in
the universe as a force for good."

Or so I explain to Tana as *21 Jump Street* goes to commercial break. She smiles brightly, unsure how seriously to take my epiphany. "You going to bogart that spliff all night?" I pass her the joint. "You're not going to join the Peace Corps," she asks, taking a puff. "Are you?"

"No," I reply, taking the weed back from her. "I don't know. I haven't thought this all the way through. But it's almost like my whole life has been leading to this point."

"You *have* spent a lot of time in the food *service* industry. And delivering pot, you're helping a lot of people."

I nod gravely, examining the burning stick in my hand. "Food for the soul."

"Uh-huh," she says, reaching toward me. "Now share. Me hungry."

Earlier that evening, I'd spoken to Larry Kirschenbaum about Daphne's father. He gave me the name of a private investigator he thought might be able to help—an ex-cop named Henry Head—but he'd probably charge me five hundred a week.

"Not a problem," I responded a little too quickly, causing Larry to study me in a new light. Not respect, exactly—more like the instinct, earned from decades of defending criminals, that I might sometime soon require his professional services.

The truth was I *could* afford Henry Head, thanks to my ongoing business relationship with Danny Carr. I'd planned to reinvest the extra salary into my ongoing efforts to woo K. away from Nate. But so far it hadn't mattered: I hadn't seen her in the nearly two weeks since we'd mashed in the bar. In the rush to leave I'd forgotten to ask for her number. Ray thought he had it, but couldn't find it, and suggested I "just drop by her place." Which I did, once again feeling like a stalker, again with zero success.

That Friday night, I debark the elevator on Danny Carr's floor. His assistant Rick is outside the office door, hovering over a fax machine.

"So if it isn't the man of mystery," he greets me.

"Howdy, Rick. The boss around?"

"Just finishing up a call. You guys gonna . . ." Rick places his thumb and forefinger in front of his mouth and sucks in, mimicking a toke.

"I haven't the slightest idea what you're talking about."

Rick smiles, or at least bares his canines trying. "So it's like that, huh?" He turns his attention to the in-box on his desk. A minute later, Danny pokes his head out from his office.

"My new best friend," he says, gesturing me in. "You can go, Rick."

"What about the fax?"

"I'll get the fax," Danny replies. "Now get out of here."

Rick gathers his things slowly, a man with something on his mind. "You decide about those tickets?" he finally blurts out.

"Yeah," Danny says in a flat voice. "I don't think that's going to happen this time."

"Ain't no thang," replies Rick. "See you on Monday, Boss. Don't party too hard this weekend. Later days and better lays."

Danny's already on his way back into his office. I follow, closing the door behind me per his request.

"What a prick," he says, already removing the vaporizer from his sin cabinet. "Wants my fucking Knicks tickets to impress some piece of tail from Staten Island. What a fucking waste of a human penis."

Danny hands me the money, five hundred dollars already promised to Henry Head, who during our five-minute telephone conversation would guarantee no immediate results but assured me that "when you need a private dick, you can count on the Head." I'd kept reminding myself that Larry Kirschenbaum had vouched for him.

"You want 'em?" he asks. "The tickets. I'm supposed to be on a plane to Saint Bart's in . . ." He looks at his watch. "Right now. Come on, take 'em. They're behind the Sonics bench. You can play bongos on the X-Man's bald head. Don't . . . You can't do that, I'll lose my tickets, but you know what I mean."

It's amazing, I tell myself as I exit the office with the tickets in my pocket, *what you can accomplish by just not being a dickhead.* And it only gets better: The elevator is waiting for me when I push the button. The uptown 2 arrives the moment I reach the platform. There is an open seat near the door. And when I finally reach the hotel with time enough to change— out of slavish loyalty to what I now consider to be my brand, the well-dressed drug dealer, I'm still wearing business-casual—I hear a familiar voice call my name. I spin around to see K.

"I thought I recognized that ass," she says.

"Hey," I protest. "I'm not just a sex object you can ogle."

"Mmm. Too bad. I had fun the other night."

"Me too. I tried to call you until I realized I didn't have your number."

"I've been super-busy," she says.

"Life in the big city."

We wait together for the light at Seventh Avenue. "Also . . . ," she starts, then trails off.

"Don't tell me. You've got herpes."

"Gross me out. No, I've got a boyfriend. And I probably shouldn't be kissing strange men in bars."

"I think if you get to know me," I say, starting across the street, "you'll find I'm really not that strange. And besides, there's the whole thousand-mile rule."

"That's *riiiight*," she says, catching up to me. "I forgot about the thousand-mile rule. I'm sure Nate would understand."

"He seems like an understanding guy."

"Only I can't ask him tonight," she adds, "on account of the band being in Cleveland. How far away is Cleveland?"

"Cleveland, Spain?"

By the time we reach the Chelsea, I have a date for the Knicks game. We agree to change and meet in the lobby in fifteen minutes.

"WEED MAN!" MY DATE CALLS to me from the end of the row. "You're our only hope!"

"Yell it a little louder, Nate," I reply. "I don't think the whole team heard you." One of the Sonics' bench players turns around and winks at me, confirming they had.

I take some solace in the idea that he's not trying to embarrass me as much as draw attention to himself—while I still don't have enough information to judge his musical talents, it's clear that Nate already has a rock star's appetite for attention. He's the only person in the Garden wearing a purple velvet Mad Hatter lid festooned with peacock feathers.

"I seem to have departed the manse without my portfolio," he continues, his voice faux-preppie, a nod and a fuck-you to the millionaires who surround us, it seems. "Would you be so kind as to slap a twenty on me? The local stout runs five a pop."

I wonder how badly we have to behave for Danny Carr to lose his season tickets. I give us a fighting chance.

After waiting for a half hour in the lobby at the hotel, staring at the art and evading Herman's questions about poems I had no intention of writing, I'd foolishly climbed up the stairs.

I find the door to K.'s suite partially open. I knock and no one answers, so I cautiously push open the door. Nate walks out of the bedroom, cradling his cock.

"Wart or canker sore?" he asks, holding it up for inspection.

Nate's dick is long, skinny, and buck naked, like everything else about him. Even from a distance I can see what appears to be a red blemish near the tip. But Nate's not looking at his dick—he's staring at the Knicks tickets, which for some idiotic reason I'm holding in my hand.

"The Knicks? Bangin'!" Nate turns toward the bedroom, mock-Ricky Ricardo. "Oh, Lucy . . . you have a *vis-i-tor*. . . ."

K. emerges from the bedroom in a robe. Her eyes plead for forgiveness. Everything else about her screams *freshly fucked*.

"Need a date?" Nate asks, referring to the tickets. "I fly home early to surprise my girl only to discover she's ditching me for the Isle of Lesbos."

"Maybe if you warned me you were coming," she says to Nate without taking her eyes off me, "I wouldn't have made plans with the girls."

"They always say they want more spontaneity," Nate says, "Until you surprise them."

"That's only because your idea of a surprise," protests K., "is to accidentally slip it into my ass."

Nate grins like a well-fed cat. "You weren't complaining for very long."

"And they say romance is dead," I deadpan, a major accomplishment given the nuclear explosions taking place in my brain.

"I like this guy," Nate tells K., whipping a tentacle-like arm around my shoulder. "So what do you say, Weed Man? Boys night out?"

I look at my pager, amazed at the speed of my transformation from would-be cuckolder to cuckold. I know I don't have any good reason to be angry at K., but I am anyway. "Why not?"

Who the hell walks into a room holding up tickets?

As Danny promised, the seats are close enough to smell the game. But smelling sweaty men hardly seems like a consolation prize. When Nate offers to buy me a beer with my own money, I pull a twenty out of my pocket, crumple it into a ball, and wing it at him.

"Classy," he says, picking it up off the floor.

I try to lose myself in the action. The game moves both faster and slower than it does on television. Up close, the players jump and cut much faster than their freakish size (also more impressive in person) should allow. But the Knicks' style of play, halting and deliberate and bruisingly predicated on fouling the opposition every time they drive toward the basket, seems to suck some of the joie de vivre from the room. Not helping is their coach, who calls a time-out every time the Sonics manage to string together two baskets in a row.

"You should see the asshole who usually sits here," I hear a guy behind me say about my seats.

A backhanded compliment? Damnation by faint praise? Does it fucking matter? I am itching for a fight.

Only when I spin around, I see Liz, my favorite client from the Upper East Side. Her attention-demanding breasts provide support to something fuzzy and charcoal, too long to be a sweater but too short to be a skirt, allowing plenty of exposure for long, athletic legs wrapped in shimmery black tights and high-heeled boots. Her hair is moussed and tousled. A light layer of makeup helps her eyes to outsparkle the diamond studs in her ears, while the string of pearls around her neck make her look like she's just stepped out of *Vanity Fair*.

"Hi," I say.

"You know this guy?" says the man sitting next to her, the one I'd targeted for a fight. He's in his mid-forties, wearing a brown suit and a Yankees cap to cover what I assume is male-pattern baldness. Liz's mind seems to be cycling through potential replies. Or potential escape routes.

"Liz and I went to high school together," I say, extending a hand. "The name's Coopersmith . . . Biff Coopersmith."

"Jack Gardner," he replies, taking my hand tentatively, then crushing it. "High school? I could swear Lizzie said she went to Spence."

"Mmm-hmm," I say, freeing my hand.

"He means summer camp," Liz interjects, "since Spence is an all-girls school."

"Summer camp!" I laugh. "She was an absolute beast during Color War."

"Coopersmith," says Jack, rubbing his chin. "No relation to Casey Coopersmith . . . ?"

"You know my cousin Casey?" I slap Jack on the knee. "He's the best."

"Casey's a she."

"Well, sure," I say. "Since the operation."

Liz, who'd been smiling wryly, allows herself a soft giggle. Nate returns with the beers and I make introductions all around. I don't bother with my ridiculous new alias as I doubt Nate remembers my real name.

"You have a lovely daughter," Nate says to Jack, nodding toward Liz and moving way up my admittedly short list of people I like. With a bullet.

"I do," Jack manages through clenched teeth. "She's thirteen and lives in Boston with her mother."

"Good for you, old man!" says Nate. Now it's his turn to slap Jack on the knee. "So the plumbing's still in order then?"

"The plumbing is in excellent condition," he replies with surprising pride. "I should know. I'm a urologist."

"You're a cock doc?" screams Nate, once again capturing the attention of the Sonics' bench. "Brilliant! You probably get this all the time, but I've got this spot on my wanker. . . ."

I look at Liz, expecting to see mortification. Instead she's biting her lip, determined to keep the giggles from becoming guffaws. "I'm going to get a pretzel," I announce, already on my feet. I've just planted myself on line when Liz appears behind me.

"Want to smoke a chonger?" she asks.

We settle on a service corridor off the upper deck. She pulls a joint out of her clutch. I do my trick with the Zippo. "You're just full of surprises, Biff," she says, blowing a cloud of smoke over her shoulder. "But thank you for not, you know, just blurting it out. It's only our third date. Too early to tell him I have my own weed dealer. Your name's not really Biff, is it?"

"Third date's a biggie. You two done the wild thing yet?"

"The wild thing?" She folds her arms. Playfully. Maybe even flirtatiously. Then again, I misread the signs with K.

"I'm not judging," I say. "We can't control who we're attracted to."

"It's not as if . . . ," she sputters. "I mean, he's handsome. . . ."

"Bald."

"Distinguished," she counters.

"Rich?"

"He is that," she sighs. "Look, you don't know me at all. . . ."

"Not yet. But I do know this. You could be doing a lot better than the Cock Doc."

Her cheeks redden. "That's sweet of you to say."

"I speak only the truth, milady. I know plenty of young bucks who'd be honored to lay their horns at your doorstep."

"I have no idea what that means. Is that supposed to be some kind of metaphor?"

"Meta-what?!" I am already buzzed. "The truth is I don't know what I'm talking about. My brain's been running low on oxygen from the minute I saw you tonight."

"You're bad," she says.

What happens next isn't a kiss, exactly. She darts in, touches her lips to mine, and pulls away.

"It'd be a shame to miss the rest of the game," I say.

Five minutes later, we're making out in the back of a cab, destination Upper East Side. Arriving at her building, I peel off another twenty and tell the cabbie to keep the change. We fast-walk into the building, trying not to giggle at the door-man.

The charade falls apart in the elevator. We're laughing. Tears stream down our faces. Then the tongue-mashing resumes. My hands are in tactile wonderland, sliding between the fuzzy sweater and the textured tights. I run my hand under her sweater, cupping her carriage. She moans and presses toward me. I risk a move to the front of her hose, gently tracing a line up her thigh. Two fingers pause between her legs. I can feel her wetness through the nylon.

The elevator opens and we stumble into the hall. Liz leads me by the hand to her apartment. She's fumbling through her clutch for the keys. I try to kiss her again but she places a finger over my lips. She unlocks the door. Inside, a redheaded girl, fourteen maybe, looks up from the TV.

"You're home early," the redhead says.

"Everything okay?" Liz asks.

"Not a peep," the redhead replies. She's already putting on her coat.

Liz thanks her and hands her some money. Double-locks the door behind her. She turns toward me like she's going to explain something, but my lips are already back on hers, my hands again finding their way below her belt. We fall onto the couch. Her hand slides inside the waist of my jeans as far as it can—I'm rock-hard and there's not exactly a lot of room to maneuver. She uses both hands to rip down my pants and boxers—problem solved. My cock springs out. She squats in front of me and runs her tongue up my shaft, beginning at the base. Reaching the tip, she stands up, satisfied at the view from above. She retrieves a condom from her clutch and tosses it to me. I wrestle with the wrapper while she wiggles out of her tights. She waits for me to finish, hand on hip, a few threads of sweater to protect her modesty.

In the next room, an infant begins to cry.

Privately I've always considered myself to have some talent for measuring a woman's mood. But the expression on Liz's face is forcing me to reconsider. Not blank, but the opposite. Regret coexisting with pride, with hints of resentment, joy, frustration, shame, resignation, and curiosity. When it comes to emotions, women know how to paint with the full set of oils, while men are busy doodling with crayons.

Liz mumbles a few words of apology and exits in the direction of the intensifying wail. I sit on the couch and look at my raging hard-on, feeling ridiculous. So I slip on my underwear, grab my pants, and beat a path for the door.

The wailing disappears—I can hear Liz whispering something soft and reassuring. Just ditching her is starting to feel like the wrong play. I look around for a telephone: I can write down her number and call her later to apologize.

"Classy," I hear Nate saying in my head.

I tiptoe into the bedroom. Having ditched the sweater, Liz sways bare in front of a vanity mirror. She's nursing a baby, sex indeterminate at this distance. The scene in the mirror confirms I'd been right about the attention-demanding breasts. But I'd missed altogether on their target audience.

Maybe I hadn't been totally full of shit during my last conversation with Tana. Maybe it's not about scoring, but about giving.

Liz looks up at the mirror, catching me grinning like Buddha. I recognize her current expression: puzzlement. I wonder if she's awed by what I imagine to be beams of pure enlightenment shooting out of my eyes, until I realize her focus is stuck on my lower chakras. I glance down at the source of the commotion. Not Buddha, but a boner, back at full mast. By the time I look up at her again, she doesn't look so puzzled anymore. Something else entirely has moved in.

Still cradling the baby, she sits down at the edge of the bed and falls slowly sideways, until mother and child are horizontal. I sit beside her, resting my hand on her arm. She scissors her legs, an invitation to complete the circuit. *Give to receive*, I think as I enter her. *Give to receive.* I thank the universe for serving up such an excellent part for me to play.

Then I get to work. There is some serious providing to be done.

10

I WAKE UP, HARDLY AN EASY FEAT given the cocoon of silky cotton sheets and a mattress forged from some fluffy polymer of the future. Louvered blinds temper the morning sun. Rich people sleep better, which might be one of the reasons why they're rich.

Liz sits on the edge of the bed, Indian style, staring at me.

"You're awake," she says. "So glad."

"Me too." I sit up, keeping the sheets over my lap. Partly I don't want to offend with my nakedness, as she's already fully dressed: jeans and a pink Oxford button-down. Mostly I'm just resistant to having to give up the luxury of the sheets. "Last night was great."

"Great?" she asks. Her tone is scolding. Last night's sex kitten in tights has clearly departed, replaced by a dour devotee of the L.L. Bean catalog. "That's what you think? Great?"

"Really great?"

"Really great? *Really great*. Good God, I've just hit rock bottom."

"I'm a little confused. Did I suck in bed?"

"No, you were fine," she says. "Better than fine. I had fun, I did. But I need someone to explain to me how I go from a date with a doctor, a very successful single doctor, a grown-up, for once in my life, who knew about Lucy and still wanted to . . . Who still seemed interested in me as something more than . . . How do I go from That Guy to sex with my teenage drug dealer?"

"I'm no psychologist, but you *were* high. We were high. Speaking of which . . . I don't know about you, but I'm a big fan of the wake-and-bake."

"I was high," Liz says.

"I don't know why, but saying it just makes you feel better, doesn't it?"

"High while I was nursing my daughter. While my teenage drug dealer fucked me from behind. I mean . . . what kind of parent does that makes me?" Liz picks up the telephone and thrusts it toward me. "Will you call Child Services? Because if you don't, I will. Lucy would be better off in a foster home."

"All right, sister. Let's take a deep breath. First of all, I'm not a teenager. I'm twenty-one."

"*Twenty-one*. Imagine that."

"Almost twenty-one-and-a-half. And while I agree, the sex plus the nursing might have been a little on the freaky side, it doesn't make you a bad parent. Trust me on this one. I know the bad parent, and lady, you're not him. We had fun last night. Everybody deserves to have—"

"You're sweet," Liz cuts me off. "Thank you *so* much. You've really helped me to see how completely fucked up and out of control my life has become. Now if you could just get dressed and get out of here, I don't need Clarinda judging me too." She exits the room.

I gather my clothes and dress quickly, passing a husky nurse—this must be Clarinda—on the way out the door. She grins at me, a gap-toothed smile that knows all about what goes on in the night. "Lady's gonna be in a good mood this morning," she says.

"I wish you were right," I say, mostly to myself, and board the down elevator. In the lobby I'm treated to an equally knowing but much less smiley look from the doorman. At college, we had called this experience "The Walk of Shame."

I hail a cab back to the Chelsea. I slink low in my seat, re-playing the night in my head, trying to freeze-frame the moment when it went all wrong. The scene I keep stopping on is me, entering K.'s apartment, tickets held high like a pea-cock's feathers.

I pay the cabbie and walk into the lobby, immediately grateful that Herman's weekend replacement is behind the desk. Manuel happily ignores me in favor of the Spanish-language soccer game on the small black-and-white. I'm half-way up the stairs to the safety of my room when I run into K.

"Ho ho," she says. "I heard you had an interesting night."

"Interesting?"

"Nate says you ditched him for some doctor's girlfriend."

She's smiling at me with a look I've seen before, generally when my rap has crashed and burned. *You're cute and I might sleep with you*, it says, *if I was a loser devoid any self-respect.* Whatever window I had with K. is now closed.

"It wasn't exactly the night I planned," I say coolly. "The night *we* planned, actually."

"You knew I had a boyfriend."

There might be some regret in the way she's said it, but I'm in no mood to see it. I can't think of anything else to say that doesn't sound desperate, vindictive, or just plain pathetic, so I continue up to my room.

Under normal circumstances, I am a big fan of the long postcoital shower. As sick as it probably sounds, washing dried sex off my body makes me feel like a man with a mustache who discovers a few crumbs from last night's delicious meal. But I don't want to think about last night anymore. Despite the unspeakable luxury of having the communal bathroom all to myself, I scrub quickly and return to my room.

The Motorola is buzzing on the bed. A Long Island number I don't recognize. I throw on some clothes, grab a handful of change, and walk downstairs to the Mexican restaurant.

"Kings Park," says the receptionist on the other end of the line, quickly clearing up the identity of the mystery caller.

"Daphne Robichaux, please." Two more quarters go into the phone before she speaks.

"Hiya!" Daphne says brightly. "How's America?"

It's a line from *Sid and Nancy*, a call-and-response we'd appropriated as our own. "Fucking boring," I finish. "Now, who are you, cheerful person, and what have you done with Daphne."

"She met fluoxetine. And let me tell you, it was love at first swallow."

Daphne's bubbly take on life in the loony bin makes it sound more like *F Troop* than *One Flew Over the Cuckoo's Nest*. I actually find myself getting envious of her life, spent with colorful characters in what sounds like a stress-free environment. Maybe not entirely stress-free—when my father finally called the police to drop the charges, they told him she still faced possible criminal prosecution—but Daphne's last conversation with Larry has her feeling confident that at least there won't be any jail time.

I've just about run out of quarters when she asks me if there's been any news about her father. I promise to call the private investigator, which I do as soon as I hang up. This conversation turns out to be a lot shorter.

"Glad you called," says Henry Head. "Why don't you swing by the office?"

The office is in the heart of Hell's Kitchen. On the second floor of a storefront promising fake IDs and Live XXX, I find the door with *Head Investigations* stenciled on the tempered glass. There is no receptionist, just the Head-man himself, leaning back in his chair, feet on the desk. He wears a tracksuit that looks more ironic than functional—Henry Head must weigh three hundred pounds. He notes my arrival, washing half a Twinkie down his throat with a Snapple. "Brunch," he explains, gesturing toward a couch splattered with mysterious stains. "Make yourself at home."

I play it safe, resting my ass against the armrest. A radiator clangs noisily in the corner, pushing the temperature about five degrees higher than comfortable. It really does feel like home.

"Do you have any idea how many Peter Robichauxs there are in the tristate area alone?" Head asks.

I shake my head.

"Me neither. Maybe someday with the computers and all that we'll have some way of knowing. Until then, we got the white pages." He holds up a weathered phone book.

My internal temperature rises to match the room. "Let me get this straight," I say. "I just paid you five hundred dollars to skim the phone book?"

"You ever hear of Occam's razor? The shortest distance between two points is a straight line."

"Actually, Occam's razor says the simplest explanation is usually the right one," I say, drawing on my single semester of philosophy.

"No shit? Then what do you call the thing about the straight line?"

"I think that's just 'the thing about the straight line.'"

He holds up his palms in mock self-defense. "I never claimed to be a scholar."

"So is Peter Robichaux in the phone book?"

"Fourteen of 'em." Head consults a spiral-bound notebook, which is encouraging. "A couple of 'em died in the five boroughs, meaning they got death certificates in Queens. I can't tell you how much easier it is when the guy you're looking for has got a death certificate."

"You think he's dead?"

"I'm just saying it's easier, is all. Anyway, I don't think any of the dead Robichauxs are your Robichaux. Too young, too old, too black. You said he was a white fella, right?"

"Glad to see you were paying attention. What about the living Robichauxs?"

Head nods and refers back to his notebook. "One's in jail upstate on a murder beef. But I don't think it's him on account of who he murdered, as in his whole family. Your girl's still alive, right?"

"She is."

"Another's in the service . . . Germany. I got a call in to him. Long-distance—you'll see when you see the bill. As for the rest . . . squadoosh." Head rubs his hands together like a magician. Another ironic gesture. "By a variety of reasonings I was able to eliminate each of the rest as potential candidates." He jams a second yellow pastry into his mouth.

"Okay, assuming that's true, where does it leave us?"

"Like I said," he manages in between bites, "I got a call in to Germany." He wipes his mouth with a handkerchief. "It's a long shot, which is why I called you here. Our investigation has reached the proverbial cross in the road."

"You mean 'fork.' "

"How's that?"

"The expression. It's 'fork in the road.'"

Head dabs his forehead with the handkerchief. "That don't sound right. Fork's got three points, maybe four. We only got two options."

"Maybe you could just tell me what they are?"

"The first is to broaden the search . . . police records, motor vehicles, God bless. If you want, I can drive up to Albany. That's where they keep track of all the other dead people. In New York, anyway. If he died in Jersey or Connecticut, that's a whole different enchilada. They got their own phone books there too. But I gotta warn you. This kind of thing could take a while." He rubs his thumb against his forefingers, letting me know that "a while" is going to cost me. "I'm not sure how deep your pockets go."

"Not very. What's the second option?"

"The second option," Head says, "is to do absolutely nothing."

I take a moment to consider these options. "I can't say I'm particularly fond of either of them," I say.

"What can I tell you? Sometimes we got to deal with the hand how it's played."

We finally agree to continue the investigation for another week, enough time at least to hear back from the Peter Robichaux in Germany. I hand Henry Head another five hundred dollars and descend back into a freezing-cold rain that wouldn't let up for a week.

11

CHRISTMAS AT THE KIRSCHENBAUMS should be a contradiction, and would be if not for Larry Kirschenbaum's pragmatism: If his clients come in all stripes of faith, then so can he. Each year, forty or so guests are treated to a ten-foot Christmas tree and sexy caterers, usually dressed as naughty elves, serving potato *latkes*. This year, the menorah will be joined by a Kwanzaa *kinara*, a nod to a medium-famous rap artist Larry successfully defended on gun possession charges. Still, out of deference to those Irish Catholics whose need to drive inevitably collides with their passion for drink—the bread and butter of Larry's practice—the event itself will probably always be called "Christmas at the Kirschenbaums."

After making my regular Friday night delivery to Danny Carr, I take the train back to the Island. It's the first time I've been home since I moved to the city. This time, no one's awake to greet me. But it feels good to sleep in my old bed. When I wake up, my mother's already in the kitchen. I sit down at the table while she makes me pancakes.

"Dad sleeping in?"

"I don't know," Mom says. "He didn't come home last night."

I'm pouring syrup on a stack of pancakes when Dad enters through the back door. He's still wearing last night's clothes. He kisses Mom, who's joined me at the table, on the top of her head. "Goddamn Harvey made me sleep at the bar," Dad says. "I told him I was fine, but you know Harv. . . ."

"I'm sure he just wanted to be sure you were safe," my mother says without looking at him. "Honey, would you please pass me the syrup?"

"What? You don't believe me? Call Harv and ask him."

"Are his phones working?" she asks.

"What do you mean, are his phones working?"

"I mean if his phones were working, then you could have called. Or called a taxi."

"Like I need this shit first thing in the morning," Dad growls.

Welcome home, kid. Fortunately Tana calls, giving me an excuse to go back to my room.

"You're coming tonight, right?" Tana asks.

"So it's true. Your basic greetings have finally become passé. Hello to you, too."

"Are you coming or what?"

"I'm here, aren't I? At my parents?"

"I'm just making sure," she says.

"Let me guess. You're having some difficulties with a representative of the gruffer sex?"

"Something like that."

Tana sounds anxious in a way I can't quite pinpoint. "Is this something that can wait? Because I can come over now."

"I won't be here. Dottie's booked us haircuts and mani-pedis. Oh yeah, and a massage."

"Sucks to be you," I say.

"I'll see you tonight." She hangs up, good-byes apparently having gone the way of hellos. I turn to head back to the freak show in the kitchen, but the circus has come to me. Dad's framed in the doorway like the maniac in a slasher flick.

"You got a minute to talk?" he asks.

"Sure," I reply. "Is this about the money you borrowed?"

"Heh," he says, closing the door behind him. "No. I'm thinking of leaving your mother."

The silence gets awkward. "Okay," I finally say.

"That's it? Okay?"

"What do you want me to say? 'Don't do it'? 'Congratulations'?"

"You've got every right to be angry. . . ."

"I'm not angry. We both know Mom deserves better than you. I'd say that I hope the bimbette is worth it, but knowing you, she's probably not."

"*Janine*. Her name is Janine. We didn't mean for it to . . ."

"Dad," I say, "I really don't give a fuck."

He stands up, looking at me as if he wants to say something else. After a false start or two, he claps me on the shoulder and exits.

I spend the rest of the morning hiding out in my room. When it's time to go to the party, my mom insists I ride in front with Dad. "And away we go," he says, starting the engine, "to another one of Larry Kirschenbaum's tax write-offs."

We finish the trip in silence, turning the car over to one of the red-suited valets Larry has hired for the occasion. Dad makes a beeline for the bar, leaving me alone with Mom. She looks pale. I want to say something, but I don't know what my father's said to her. "Go mingle," she tells me. I give her a hug and wander into the living room.

I'm scanning the crowd for Tana when one of the Naughty Elves appears beside me. Black hair, maybe thirty, with a mole above her lip like Cindy Crawford. Not quite as tall, but she earns major points for her costume: I had no idea elves wore fishnet stockings.

"*Sufganiot?*" she asks. Her voice is husky. I can imagine her, thirty years from now, playing canasta with a long brown cigarette dangling from her mouth. Strangely, I don't find this a turnoff.

"*Gesundheit,*" I reply.

"It's a jelly donut."

I should admit that hooking up with one of the Kirschenbaum elves has long been a fantasy of mine. In the past, they've seemed remote and unattainable, like supermodels. But now that I've spent a little time next to supermodels, an elf from the Island doesn't feel like such a stretch. "If I were

Santa," I say, accepting a donut, "I don't think I'd let you out of the workshop."

She's already moving away with the tray. "Be careful," she says over her shoulder. "Bad boys usually wind up with coal in their stocking."

"What was that?" asks Tana, who at some point has materialized behind me.

"Just me figuring out what I want for Christmas this year."

"Uh, hi," she says, annoyed that I haven't bothered to turn around. My jaw drops open when I do.

"Holy shit," I say. "Look at you."

Tana is definitely something to look at. A short black cocktail dress makes the most of her already formidable cleavage. And heels. Tana *never* wears heels. "Who are you trying to impress? Is Bono coming this year?"

"You could just tell me I look great," she says.

"You look great. But you could have just looked around the room and gotten the same opinion." Indeed, most of the heads are turned her way, their faces forming a continuum between "sneaking glance" and "drooling stare."

Tana blushes. "I need a drink," she says.

A few minutes later, armed with spiked eggnogs, we settle into the couch for what's become an annual Christmas tradition for Tana and me: taking turns guessing the sins of each of the guests. "International terrorist," I say of a man with a pencil-thin mustache.

"Not even close," replies Tana. "That's Mr. Atkins. Tax evasion. What about the guy over there in the red sweater?"

I see Red Sweater but my eyes keep going until they reach my father. Scotch generally keeps my Dad in one of two states—*loose* or *too loose*—but right now he just looks uncomfortable.

He's glancing nervously at a frosted blonde in a business suit on the other side of the room. She isn't a head-turner, but she's attractive. She's standing next to a tubby, balding guy in a brown Christmas tree sweater. He has his hand wrapped around her waist. They're talking to another couple, smiling. She looks sidelong at Tubby, making sure his attention is on the other couple, then throws a half-smile across the room to my father. I'm not exactly sure how I know, but I'm sure this is Janine.

"Your ten o'clock," I say to Tana. "I think it's the trollop Dad's leaving my mom for."

Tana whips around to face me. "Excuse me?!" I quickly bring her up to speed on the morning's conversation.

"What a fucking prick!" she says, jumping off the couch.

"Where are you going?"

"To find out who she is." And then she's parting the crowd, making her way toward the two couples. I watch her introduce herself. So does my father, who looks at me with an expression teetering between anger and confusion. I toast him with my glass, which I discover is empty. Rising from the couch, I return to the bar and order a scotch. Dottie, who is talking to my mother, calls me over.

"I've just been hearing all about your job," fawns Dottie.

"And living in the city. Maybe you can help my Tana find a job when she finally finishes college."

"She's got your looks, Dottie. She doesn't need my help."

"Oh you," Dottie says, patting my arm like a frisky cat. My mother, in contrast, looks glassy-eyed.

"You all right, Ma?" I ask.

She doesn't respond. Dottie zooms in. "Judy?"

Mom jerks awake. "I'm fine," she says. "I just need some water."

"Come on," says Bonnie, taking her by the arm. "I've got some of that Evian in the kitchen."

I look for Tana. She's been cornered by the medium-famous rapper, but isn't complaining. "*Koki?*" asks a familiar husky voice.

"Now you're just making shit up," I say, turning to find the sexy elf.

She smiles. "Kwanzaa food. I believe it's made out of peas."

"I'll stick to scotch," I say, raising my glass. "I guess we're going to have to find some other way to celebrate Kwanzaa."

"Like what?" she asks.

Tana darts over before I can reply, grabbing one of the appetizers off the tray. "I'll try some of that." The sexy elf smiles and moves along.

"That, little girl, was a *koki*-block," I say to Tana when I'm sure the elf is out of earshot.

"Her?" Tana snorts. "Please."

"Whatever. So what do you know?"

"I know that J-Bigg plays all his own instruments." Tana looks across the room at the rapper. J-Bigg catches her looking and smiles. Several of his teeth are capped with gold.

"I'll bet," I reply. "Did he ask you to play his skin flute?"

Tana shoves me. "What is wrong with you?!"

"Maybe I'm jealous."

"You should be. He said we could '*roll* together.'"

"Look at you," I say. "Already part of his crew. One of his hos. Now what did you find out about Frosty the Snowlady?"

"You were right. Her name's Janine Canterbury or something like that. Married to Ted Canterwhatever, he of the hideous sweater. I mean, a brown Christmas tree? That's wack."

"Did my dad invite her here?"

"Doubt it. She seemed to know Larry," Tana says, adding when I raise an eyebrow: "In a professional way."

"My mom seems really out of it," I say, looking around the room for her. She hasn't returned from the kitchen.

"Do you think she knows?" asks Tana.

I shrug. "Hey . . . didn't you have something important to talk to me about tonight?"

"Later," she says. "When did you switch to scotch? I feel like I'm falling behind."

We're on our way to the bar when Dottie stops us. Mascara running down her face. Two minutes later I'm upstairs, yelling for my father, ripping open doors. I finally find Dad in Dottie's cedar closet, where he and Janine are making out like a couple of teenagers. He raises his hands in frustration. Janine brushes down the front of her hiked-up dress.

"Well," Dad says, "this isn't the way I wanted you two to meet." Janine, following his cue, extends a hand. I ignore it.

"It's Mom," I say. "She just collapsed in the kitchen. There's an ambulance on the way."

12

MY FATHER AND I HAVE TAKEN UP
semipermanent residence in the waiting
room at the Nassau University Medical
Center. We try to keep our conversations limited to the de-
clining fortunes of the New York Islanders and order-taking
as we alternate trips to the hospital cafeteria and replenish
cigarettes. A blurry parade of doctors keeps us apprised of my
mother's condition. The television in the visitors' room tells
us when Christmas Day has come and gone.

At the outset, my mother's condition confounds the staff.
Her lead physician, Dr. Winfield Edgars—"Call me Dr. Win,
everyone else does"—pulls no punches in his initial diagnosis: "What troubles me is that her symptoms strongly suggest
a brain tumor." I soon learn that the troubling part for Dr.
Win isn't my mother's worsening condition, but the lack of
any evidence to support his diagnosis. Despite a battery of

tests and scans, the tumor stubbornly refuses to present itself.

On the fourth day Dr. Win enters the room with a smile. "She doesn't have a tumor," he says. His voice can barely contain his excitement as he explains how her symptoms had fooled him. "Paraneoplastic syndrome. A few years ago, we wouldn't have been able to diagnose this thing. We're still not exactly sure how it works. Her brain—actually, her nervous system—is being attacked by an immune response to something else. What we're seeing in her brain are the symptoms, not the underlying cause. We had to go back and figure out what was triggering the immune response."

"And?" my father asks.

Dr. Win beams. "Lung cancer," he says.

"She doesn't even smoke," I say.

"Does she live with a smoker?" he asks, seemingly oblivious to Dad's nicotine-stained teeth and fingers. "Could also be asbestos. How old's your house?"

Dr. Win's work is done. We're turned over to Dr. Best in Oncology, who's as warm as Dr. Win, only without the sense of humor. "Ninety percent of these cases don't make it past five years," he begins, before launching into a vivid description of the aggressive radiation therapy she's about to endure.

I want to cry. I suspect my father does as well. Out of respect for unspoken family tradition, we won't do it in front of each other.

My mother's emotional state varies with her treatment schedule. But the feeling I get from her more than any other feels an awful lot like relief. She insists that I return to work. "Get back to your life. It's not healthy for you to be here."

So I do. Despite the crappy winter weather, the city feels crowded and alive. It's almost New Year's Eve, so the preppies and college kids are home from school. Business is brisk, for which I'm grateful. The constant motion helps to keep me numb.

The week I took off from work to be at the hospital and Danny Carr's current three-week vacation to Florida have conspired to wreck my personal finances, forcing me back on my subsistence diet of hot dogs and pizza. I'm definitely going to be late on my January rent, so I avoid Herman by using the fire escape to get to and from my room. I'm also ignoring Henry Head, lest he hit me with a bill.

Tana pages me every day. Most of the time I don't call her back. I'm just not up for talking. But she breaks down my resistance with the offer of a home-cooked meal, delivered to my room at the Chelsea. I meet her at Penn Station, where she debarks the train carrying two steaming aluminum trays and a small Igloo cooler. "Homemade ice cream," she says. "We can pick up a bottle of wine on the way back to your place. Is Chardonnay okay? I think it will pair well with the chicken." She's apparently joined a wine-appreciation club at college.

We stop for the wine and plastic cutlery, as I have no silverware. Tana dishes out the servings onto paper plates. When she produces two candles from her jacket, I raid the communal bathroom for two rolls of toilet paper to use as holders. We light the candles and toast with plastic cups. I dig greedily into the meal. Tana makes up for my lack of conversation with a series of thoughtful questions about my mother, which I answer mainly with nods and shrugs. "How about your dad?" she asks. "Is he still going to leave her for Janine?"

"I don't have any idea," I confess, having temporarily broken from the meal for a cigarette next to the open window.

"Aren't you freezing? You're not going to want any ice cream."

It dawns on me for the first time that Tana is wearing makeup, as she had at the Christmas party. And while she hasn't repeated the dramatic cleavage, she still looks good in designer jeans and a tight sweater that doesn't hide her curves. "I do declare, Miss Kirschenbaum, that someday you're going to make one of those sorry excuses for men you like to date a very, very happy camper."

Tana sighs. "I'm so done with sorry excuses for men."

I lift my cup. "Here, here. To muff-diving." She laughs, spitting out some of her wine. I tear off a piece of one of the candleholders and hand it to her.

"At least I'd be getting some," she says.

"Come on. It's not that bad, is it?" I ask. Her expression is half-quizzical. And half something else. "How bad is it?"

"You know I've never gone all the way, right?"

"With a woman? Hey, homosexuality's not for everyone."

"I mean with anyone."

"Wai . . . Wha . . . Never?"

"I was kind of thinking," she says, her voice barely a whisper, "that maybe it should be you who initiates me."

A thought pops into my brain. "The other night, when you said you wanted to talk to me . . ." She nods shyly. I've never seen Tana so vulnerable. I pull her close for a hug, and another thought creeps into my head.

Oh. So close. *But.*

"First of all," I say, "I'm incredibly flattered. . . ."

"Oh God," says Tana. She's already pushing away from me. "Here we go."

"You're taking this the wrong way. You are a brilliant, incredibly sexy woman, Tana Kirschenbaum. But you're also my sister—maybe not by blood, but you know what I mean. Sex for me is . . ."

I stop. I don't have any idea how to finish the sentence. What does sex mean to me? Why don't I want to have it with Tana?

She's cleaning up dinner. "I can do that," I say. Tana puts down a plate and grabs her coat off the bed. "Can we talk about this?"

She's putting on her jacket. "There isn't anything to talk about," she says. "You're right. Bad idea. Totally retarded."

"I don't remember saying any of those things."

She's walking out the door. "I should go."

"Can I at least walk you to the station?" I follow after her, hoping the cold air will clear my head and let me undo whatever damage I've done. She pauses in the hallway, waiting for me to catch up.

But she changes her mind the moment we reach the street. "You know what? It's too cold. I'll just get a cab." Tana flags a cab before I can offer a counterargument.

"Thanks for dinner."

"Tell your mom I'm going to come see her," Tana says. Then she closes the door and the cab pulls away.

13

I HAVE NO INTEREST IN RETURNING to the coffin I call home and besides, I'm feeling pretty goddamn sorry for myself. At times like these, there's really no substitute for getting good and drunk. Out of convenience, I choose the Mexican place next door.

I'm throwing back my first shot of tequila when I remember I'm still broke. I find a ten in my pocket, money I've budgeted for the weekend's food. I work through the math—spacing out the leftovers from Tana's meal, I should survive through Monday. So now I've got three shots and a tip. Enough for a buzz, maybe, but not quite the obliteration I'd been hoping for.

By the time the third shot is blazing down my food pipe, I'm pouring my troubles out to the bartender. Ernesto from Nicaragua. Who is, right now, the wisest man in the world.

"So what can you tell me, Ernesto? That I'm an idiot? That love is impossible? That I'm a stupid gringo whose problems don't amount to a hill of beans?"

"Ah." Ernesto nods sagely. "*Dios nos odia todos.*"

"That's pretty," says a voice from behind me. It's K. She looks like she's been crying. "What does it mean?"

"I'm pretty sure he said that 'God hates us all.' But I flunked Spanish so who knows for sure. Are you okay?"

"I'm fine," she replies. "Just fine. Nate and I broke up."

I've just broken my best friend's heart. My mother is dying in the hospital while my father cheats on her with a bottle blonde. Yet the news from K. makes me bite my lip to keep from smiling. "Well, pull up a seat, lady. The lonely hearts club is in session."

"Why?" asks K. "What's going on with you?" I bring her up to speed about Tana and my mother, adding that I'm too broke to get drunk. "You poor baby," she says. "Let me take care of you."

We order another round of drinks from Ernesto, who frankly looks relieved to be done with me. I tell K. about the Christmas party and the hospital. She tells me about her breakup with Nate.

She'd been offered what she called an "obscene" amount of money for two weeks of shoots in Southeast Asia. Victoria's Secret was starting a new ad campaign there and K., as it turned out, still had a devoted following among red-blooded Asian men. She'd intended to turn the job down—the money would be nice, but she didn't *need* it, and did she really want to go back to the loneliness, even if it was only for two weeks? But when she told Nate about the offer, he freaked out. Taking advantage of Scott the Drummer's winter break, Venomous Iris planned to take up residence in the studio for as long as it took to finish the album. Nate insisted he needed her for emotional support. But after one day in the studio, she realized that her real job was to remind them to eat in the midst of a collective heroin binge and, when supplies ran low, to score some more.

"I mean, I'm not a fucking drug dealer," she says.

"Thanks," I reply with the appropriate sarcasm.

"You're different," she says. "Pot's not a drug. It's a survival tool. Anyway, he said that if I wouldn't do it, he could find some other slut who would. And that maybe he'd finally get a decent blow job. Can you believe him?"

"What an asshole," I say.

"What an asshole," she says.

An hour later, K. and I are having sex in my room. It's drunk and sloppy and I'm not really sure that I'm not dreaming the whole thing until I wake up the next morning and she's still there. Then she wakes up and we do it again, almost completely curing my hangover.

We walk glove-in-mitten down the street to a French bistro. K. insists on paying for the eggs Benedict and Bloody Marys. "A hard-luck case" is how she describes me to the waiter, but the food's restorative powers temper any injury to my masculine pride. We return to my room, where, this time, we get it right. The sex begins tenderly, the mystery of the new mixed with an intimacy that's just starting to feel familiar, and ends athletically, our two bodies moving like pistons.

Now we're holding hands on the elevator, our fingers intertwined. We ride to the fourteenth floor, where Roscoe Trune's annual New Year's Eve party is under way. There is no official ownership of rooms at the Chelsea, but the suite might as well belong to Roscoe, an openly gay poet from Savannah, Georgia, who's resided there for almost as long as I've been alive. K., the invited guest, is greeted with kisses on each cheek; I'm treated cordially, but with the subtly raised eyebrows that benefit the arrival of a scandalous home-wrecker. They'd expected to see Nate.

The exception is Ray, who eyes me with a newfound respect. "I've got to hand it to you," he tells me. "I didn't think anyone was breaking that ice." The pupils of his eyes look like Oreo cookies. I'll later find out that he—along with most of the party—is on something called "Adam," a psychedelic that by the time I get around to trying it, a few years later, is better known as "Ecstasy." What I know now is that every conversation seems to wind up with someone rubbing my sleeves to feel the texture or offering a non sequitur commentary on the shine of my hair. Undue credit, I think, for a guy who simply hasn't bothered to shower.

Later, while K. dances with a shirtless, muscled man who Ray reassures me is "one of Roscoe's boy toys," he proposes that I join him on a weekend trip to South Korea. "I'm going to see a goddess," Ray says.

"You're on drugs, Ray. Try to keep it on Earth for us in the cheap seats."

"I shit you not, man. She's a real live goddess."

"Really? Does she ride a unicorn?"

"She's a *Kumari*, man. A bodily incarnation of the goddess Taleju."

"Tally who?"

"Taleju. It's the Nepalese name for the goddess Durga. A total bad-ass. Like, she's got ten arms and carries swords and shit. She rides a fucking tiger."

"I'll admit that the ten arms present some interesting possibilities, but take it from me: Women and sharp objects, they do not mix well."

Ray claps his hands. "I'm not saying she *is* Durga. The point is that Devi—that's her name, Devi—was chosen from like thousands of girls to be Durga's earthly incarnation."

"Kind of like the Miss Universe pageant," I suggest.

"Exactly! Only a lot more hard-core. She had to have what they call 'the Thirty-Two Perfections.' A voice as soft and clear as a duck's. A chest like a lion. A neck like a conch shell."

"Every time I start to take you seriously, I remember you're on drugs."

"I am being totally serious, man. For ten years, her feet were not allowed to touch the ground. Some dudes carried her everywhere in one of those, you know, canopy things. People lined up to touch them—her fucking feet!—for good luck. Even the king of Nepal, once a year he got down on his knees and kissed those hoofers."

"And you think she'll slum with a mortal like you?"

"That's the best part. She's not technically a goddess any-more. *Taleju* means 'virgin.' Once she, you know, *bleeds*, the gig is up—Durga's got to find herself a new host. And Devi? One day she's a goddess, the next she's a woman with serious self-esteem issues. Or what I like to call my wheelhouse!"

"You're kind of a fucked-up guy, Ray."

"I know. But what can I do?" He grins evilly. "How'd we get started on Devi?"

"You were going to Korea . . ."

"Korea!"

". . . to see a goddess from Nepal who . . . Why is she in Korea again?"

"She's a model. Vicky's hired her for the same campaign as K. Which is why *we're* going to Korea. You can surprise her. Chicks love that shit. It overloads their brain so much that they can only think with their pussies."

"As tempting as it might be to turn K. into a drooling sex zombie, I don't exactly have the fundage for international jet-setting."

"Nobody pays for travel. You can fly for free."

"No, *you* fly for free. You're a photographer. Drug dealers pay full fare."

"You go as a courier. There are a bunch of places down-town that will hook you up. You find someone that needs something delivered to Korea, and they pay for the trip."

"A courier? Doesn't exactly sound like it's on the up-and-up."

Ray laughs. "Didn't you just say you were a drug dealer?"

"The redistribution of certain herbal products is one thing. International smuggling, that's an entirely different cup of tea. I take it you've never seen *Midnight Express*?"

"I'm talking about legitimate businessmen. A buddy of mine does it all the time. Important documents—contracts and shit. You take ten minutes to drop them off, the rest of the trip is free."

"Isn't it, like, a ten-hour flight?" I say. My resistance is starting to soften. "I can't exactly ask for any more time off from work."

"Ten hours? More like twenty."

"I've got to be back on Monday. Unless I'm missing something, a day there and a day back leaves me zero time there."

"You're missing something," he says with a stupid grin. "The international date line."

"Spell it out for a college dropout who's never been farther than Canada?"

"You've got to fly across the date line, which, I don't know exactly how, but it turns back time. You leave Korea at six o'clock Monday morning, you get back to New York at six o'clock Monday morning. Maybe even earlier."

"That doesn't sound possible."

"Neither did you nailing K. But look what happened." We both turn toward the dance floor. K. catches us looking at her and smiles back, rolling her eyes at her partner's enthusiastic interpretation of MC Hammer.

A few minutes before midnight Roscoe throws open the

windows. I'm finally in a room with balconies, à la *Sid and Nancy*. The cold air is bracing, but thick with anticipation rising from the millions of revelers in the streets. Good-bye, 1980s; the '90s have got to be an improvement. K. finds my hand and holds on to it, and when the clock strikes twelve, we engage in a very public display of affection. A few minutes later, we return to my room and do a few more things in private.

14

NEW YEAR'S DAY TURNS OUT TO BE work as usual, or unusual, as the Motorola buzzes all day. Everyone in New York City has a hangover to nurse, and it's on me to play Doctor Feelgood. I reluctantly leave K. in my bed and try to lose myself in the flow.

I probably would have forgotten all about Ray's proposed adventure if chance hadn't intervened.

A lot of artists take crap for their "creative temperament," and probably rightly so. But in a city like New York, the cost of living requires its starving artists to be true pioneers: It takes real guts to settle the kinds of neighborhoods where most right-thinking folks would soil their pants if they were caught there past sundown. That's what I'm thinking, anyway, as a delivery to a metal sculptor south of Houston leads me through what not too long ago must have felt like a combat zone. Only now I see trendy boutiques popping up like weeds through the cracks in the sidewalks. Maybe art really can change the world.

After the Meet-Up, I pass a travel agency that looks like it caters to the NYU crowd. An easel in front lists international fares to exotic cities that sound only vaguely familiar. Where the hell is Machu Picchu? Christchurch? I know from a music video that a night in Bangkok can "make a hard man humble," but that doesn't mean I could find it on a globe. Seoul, Korea, is about three-quarters of the way down the list and, at $599, well out of financial reach. But a sign in the window promises passport photos, immunization cards, and air courier jobs. Ten minutes, five missed pages, and ninety-nine dollars later, I leave the agency with instructions to pick up an expedited passport and to meet a Mr. Yi, this Friday night at eight P.M., in front of the Korean Air desk at Kennedy's International Terminal. The agent warns me not to be late. "Mr. Yi is a stickler for schedule."

The night before K. departs, we go out for a farewell dinner in the West Village. It's a nook on Barrow Street, the kind of place that only last week I would have mocked without mercy, full of violins and suggestive artwork to serve up manufactured romance for moneyed stiffs lacking passion or originality. Instead, I feel myself smiling along with the rest of the suckers as two couples become engaged before we've had a chance to see the menu. After dinner, K. and I walk back to the hotel. She wraps her arm in mine and leans against my shoulder like an old lover. I feel like I'm floating in a warm bath of endorphins. Less cynically, I am falling in love.

"I can't believe I'm leaving tomorrow," she says later, from our postcoital cuddle. "I don't want to leave you alone." I want to tell her everything: about my surprise trip; about my feelings for her. But then she climbs on top of me for another round. "I'm just going to have to exhaust you before I go."

When I wake the next morning, she's already left for the airport. A funny and sentimental note promises more good times upon her return. Then my pager buzzes, another unfamiliar number from Long Island. It turns out to be Danny Carr.

"Welcome back, Danny. How was Florida?"

"Too much snow," Danny replies, clearly not meaning precipitation. "A lot of fake tits. When did that happen? Not that I'm complaining. A lot of girls, it makes them fuckable, you know? I need double this week."

"Double? I don't know that I can even give you the regular. You didn't exactly tell me when you were coming back."

"You've got to think ahead, man. Look, I'll pay you *triple*."

"Even if I could, Danny, I don't have that kind of money to lay out for you."

"Quadruple. Come meet me in Bridgehampton and I'll front you what you need."

I call Billy and tell him that I can't make it in to work, using my mother as an excuse. An hour later, I'm on the train to Long Island, continuing past Levittown to the Hamptons. I exit to

weather cold and unbeachlike and take a taxi to the address
Danny gave me. When I ring the doorbell, I'm greeted by a distinguished old man who might have been the butler, had he
been wearing something more than a banana hammock.

"Yello!" I say, startled by the sight of so much wrinkled
skin.

"*Hallo!*" says the old man. He speaks with a heavy accent,
German I think. "You are him? You are older than I ask for."

"Uh, I think I might have the wrong house."

"Take it easy, Hans," says Danny, who appears behind him
wearing, I'm thankful to see, a much more modest bathing
suit. "Go back to the sauna. I'll let you know when the entertainment arrives."

Hans frowns and disappears into the back of the house,
but not quickly enough for me to save my eyes from confirming that, yes, his swimsuit is a thong. "Fucking Germans,"
Danny says. "You wouldn't believe the things I've got to do to
keep them happy. Thanks for coming all the way out here.
Normally I'd make Rick do it, but dickweed has the week off.
You want a drink or a bump? I've got the Bolivian."

I point over my shoulder. "The cab's waiting for me."

"Right, right, right, right," says Danny. He disappears into
the back of the house, returning a moment later with three
thousand dollars in cash.

The rest of the week is a blur. My imaginary smokers are
inhaling like chimneys as I scramble to put together ten extra
bags for Danny. There's a return trip to the agency to pick up
my passport. A guilty phone call to my mother, although her

mood brightens considerably when I hint at a female presence in my life.

By Friday afternoon, just a few hours before my flight to Korea, I've managed to pull together the package for Danny. I load my jacket with more than two pounds of weed and take the train downtown. When I reach Danny's building, the security guard is away from the desk. Smirking, I sign myself in as "Mr. Green" and board the elevator.

When the doors open again, I'm looking at two policemen.

Every instinct I have tells me to run. But the simple geometry of the elevator box dictates otherwise. Besides, they're looking right at me.

"It's okay," one of them says. "It ain't a bomb or nothing."

I plaster on what I hope is a convincing smile. My rapidly escalating body temperature feels like it might ignite the two pounds of marijuana in my jacket, whose unmistakable aroma, I'm certain, is wafting up through my collar. I am definitely going to jail.

I'm not really conscious of walking down the hallway, but suddenly I'm in front of Rick's desk. I haven't evaded the storm but sailed right into its epicenter: Danny's office is awash with blue uniforms.

In contrast to my own internal horror show, Rick looks relaxed, maybe even wide-eyed, like we're watching actors film an episode of a TV cop show. He's about to say something else when Danny gets escorted from his office, a sober man in a gray suit attached to each arm.

Danny looks through me as if I'm not there, a gesture I quickly find myself grateful for. "Mark my words, Ricky," he says to his assistant. "I'm going to fuck you."

"You might want to save some of the romance for your cellmate," Rick replies.

Danny cackles. "What cellmate? You think I'm going to wind up in prison? Worst-case scenario is a country club vacation, you dumb, ignorant fuck-face."

"I wouldn't be so sure about that," says another sober-suited man, defined by his posture and attitude as the Man in Charge. He holds Danny's vaporizer in his hand. "I've already identified at least three Class A narcotics in that cabinet of yours back there. Your white collar's gonna look a lot dirtier to the judge. Hope you got a good lawyer, Danny." The Man in Charge turns to one of the uniforms. "Clear off one of these desks, willya? Lay out the drugs and the paraphernalia. The *Post* will want a picture." Then he turns to me. "Who the hell are you?"

There are a lot of ways to answer the question, and none of them seem good. "You know this guy?" he asks Danny.

"I don't know anything," Danny says defiantly. "From here on out you're talking to lawyers." He mimes the act of zipping his mouth and throwing away the key.

"Get him out of here," says the Man in Charge, sniffing the air. "Mother Mary and Joseph. The whole floor smells like grass." He returns to Danny's office, leaving me face-to-face with Rick.

"I don't think Danny's going to be able to take your meeting," Rick says. "Let me walk you to the elevator."

Rick is bursting to share. "Those Germans he kept meet-ing?" he says as soon as we're out of earshot of the police. "Fronting money from Iran. Fucking communists."

I resist the urge to tell him Iran's a theocracy. "Crazy," I say instead.

"Whatever. Hey, I know you were his drug dealer, but as far as I'm concerned, the drugs were incidental. Live and let live, right? Fucking weed. Who smokes fucking weed any-more? Now if you could score me some blow. . . ."

I glance at the various law enforcers still milling about the office, mercifully oblivious to our conversation. "I don't . . ."

"Don't have any idea what I'm talking about. Whatever. Play it your way. Happy New Year."

"See you around, Rick," I say, managing to wedge myself into the elevator.

"He got what was coming to him!"

"Nobody gets what's coming to them," I say as the doors slide shut. "And what they do get they probably didn't de-serve," I add, aloud, to no one.

I fast-walk for maybe a dozen blocks, looking nervously over my shoulder, but I don't think I'm being followed. I hail a cab.

"Kennedy," I say, climbing in. It's already almost six o'clock, two hours until my meeting with Mr. Yi. "How long do you think it will take?"

The cabbie, a burly guy with an unpronounceable name, examines me with glazed eyes. "Depends on traffic," he says, nearly slamming into a parked car. He spits a series of what must be profanities in a foreign language, something Eastern European.

Are you okay?" I ask.

He grunts. "Double shift."

"Just get us there in one piece."

"You don't like, you find other cab," he says, turning around to face me.

"Can you keep your eyes on the—" Too late. I hear a sickening screech as the cab scrapes against a parked car. The cabbie throws the wheel in the other direction, overcompensating enough to slam into a town car in the next lane. I'm thrown forward, then sideways as the cabbie pulls the wheel the other way, sending the car into a spin. We bounce off two more cars before coming to a stop, facing oncoming traffic. Several more cars collide around us.

We sit for a minute in silence. "I'm going to find that other cab now," I tell him, hopping out of the backseat and sprinting to the safety of the sidewalk. Traffic on First Avenue has come to a complete halt.

"The fare!" he screams after me, climbing out of the cab with what looks like a police baton. I flip him the bird and scramble over the hood of the dented town car. I sprint two long blocks to the next uptown avenue and stop another cab.

"Kennedy," repeats my new driver, a turbaned Pakistani who at least doesn't seem dangerously fatigued. "Do you want we take the tunnel or the bridge?"

"Which is faster?"

He shrugs. "That is not for me to decide."

"Which is *usually* faster?"

"Sometimes the bridge, sometimes the tunnel."

"Okay, the tunnel."

"I think maybe the bridge is faster."

"Fine," I say. "The bridge."

The taxi pulls up to JFK's International Terminal ten minutes past my appointed meeting time with Mr. Yi. "We should have taken the tunnel," says the cabbie. "You never know, you know what I'm saying, man?"

"How much?"

"Forty-two dollars." I toss three twenty-dollar bills at the cabbie. "You don't have change?" When I shake my head no, he sighs. He makes a show of fumbling through his pockets. "I hope you're not in a hurry!"

"Well played," I tell him. I leap out of the cab, leaving him a nearly 50 percent tip.

"God bless you!" he yells.

As promised, the punctual Mr. Yi is nowhere to be found. "Fuuuuuck!" I scream at no one in particular.

"Watch the language," warns a passing transit cop.

By the time I've paged Mr. Yi over the public-address system and called the courier agency—both misses—the flight is less than an hour away. I slump to the floor near the ticket counter. *You'll see her again in a couple of weeks*, I say to myself. I rest my head in my hands.

"Are you okay?" asks a woman from behind the ticket counter. She's Korean, approaching middle age, dressed in the uniform of the airline I'm supposed to be flying.

"My mother is dying," I say, surprising myself.

Suddenly, we're both crying. "And you missed your flight?" she asks, holding out a tissue box.

"I was supposed to meet the guy with my tickets here, but my cab got into an accident and I was late." I accept a tissue and dab my eyes. My conscious brain is no longer in control of my speech. "She's in the hospital in Seoul . . . ," I hear myself saying. I'll spare you the rest of the performance; suffice to say that it's desperate, shameless, and in the end, effective.

"There is one thing I can do for you," she says. "The flight is not full. I could sell you a seat."

"I don't have much money."

"I can charge you bereavement fare, because of your mother. Can you afford three hundred and fifty dollars?" I nod that I can—I still have nearly a thousand dollars left over from my aborted deal with Danny. After checking my passport, she scribbles a series of numbers and letters onto my ticket. "When do you want to come back?"

"Monday morning?"

"So little time!" she says, pausing to look at me. I nod gravely with puppy-dog eyes. She begins to cry again. "There's one last thing," she adds, tears streaking down her cheeks. "I can only get you a ticket in first class."

A minute later I'm sprinting through the airport like O. J. Simpson in that Hertz commercial, arriving at the gate just before it closes. I show my ticket to a stewardess, who ushers me to a large leather chair that would have been too big to fit in my apartment.

"Cocktail?" she asks.

And then we're taking off. We're in the air for nearly an hour before an old lady sitting next to me offers me a huge smile. "Don't you just love these international trips?" she says. "So exciting. Even the air on the plane smells different. It reminds me of my garden."

I take a whiff of the air. It suddenly dawns on me that what she's smelling is the two pounds of marijuana I'm still carrying on my person. I excuse myself for the bathroom, where I flush two thousand dollars' worth of drugs down the toilet.

15

"WHERE IS YOUR LUGGAGE?" ASKS THE Korean customs official with a cherub's face.

"No luggage," I reply, causing the cherub to raise an eyebrow. "I'm only here for the weekend. To see my girlfriend."

"Ah, *girlfriend*," he says, stamping my passport. "She must be good girlfriend for all this travel."

"She's the best." I look up at the clock behind him, which places the local time at three P.M.

The cherub returns my passport and nods at the soldier who stands between me and the exit. "Soldier" isn't the right word to describe a kid with greasy hair and a soft layer of stubble and who, despite the ominous-looking machine gun hanging from his neck, reminds me of a teddy bear. He smiles and gestures at me with the gun, indicating that it's okay to pass. South Korea may be the most adorable country on Earth.

Unlike New York, Seoul's subway runs right into the airport, making it an obvious choice for a budget traveler like
yours truly—I only have a few hundred dollars left to my
name, and it is going to have to last given the abrupt end to
my relationship with Danny Carr. So I'm disappointed to discover, studying the map on the wall, that none of the stops are
labeled "the Four Seasons," K.'s hotel and the only point of reference I've bothered to bring along. One more thing to remember the next time I make a mad dash across the world to
evade the police and spend the weekend with a lady.

I exit the terminal to a sunless afternoon that feels ten degrees colder than what I've left behind. Rain is inevitable.
Luckily, the taxi stand is where I expect it to be, just outside
baggage claim, and a black-suited man escorts me into the
back of a waiting car. Ahead looms a skyline, white, shiny,
and clean, like a miniature Manhattan by way of *The Jetsons*.

About forty minutes later, we pull into a semicircular
driveway in front of the Four Seasons. The driver points to
the meter, which has just broken 11,000.

I rub my eyes to make sure I'm reading the meter correctly.
I hold up the portrait of Andrew Jackson. "*Hothyel,*" says the
cabbie. I'm saved when a smartly uniformed valet opens my
door for me. "Welcome to the Four Seasons," he says in perfect
English. "The concierge will be happy to help you exchange
your American currency for our Korean *won*. I will ask your
driver to shut off the meter while he waits. You should know
that in Korea it is not customary to tip the driver."

The doors to the hotel part like curtains, exposing an in-

ternational casting call for beauty and wealth. As I scan the
lobby for the concierge, I find Ray. He's sitting on a couch,
looking completely at home, his attention focused on a dark-
haired woman. He doesn't look up as I cross the room to the
front desk.

An agreeably efficient concierge magically transforms
$100 American into a princely 70,000 *won*. I'm on my way
back to pay the cabbie when Ray intercepts me by the door.

"There he is!" he yells, capturing me in a bear hug. "Man,
do we have to talk!"

I disentangle myself and place a hand on his shoulder.
"Good to see you, too. Just let me go settle my tab."

Outside, the cabbie accepts the exact fare on the meter
with the same smile he's worn the entire trip. I slip a 5,000-
note to the helpful valet—the extra zeros have me rolling like
Donald Trump. I reenter the hotel, this time with a strut in
my step.

Ray is waiting for me, his arm around the dark-haired
woman. I decide that thirty-two perfections might have been
an understatement, wondering if "skin like mocha ice cream"
and "the legs of a Rockette" had been among them. "You must
be Devi," I say, extending my hand. She hands me hers as if
she wants me to kiss it, which I do. "First time I've ever kissed
a goddess."

Devi flashes a perfect smile and surprises me with an ele-
gant British accent. "In my country, it is considered to be
good luck."

"This is very good news," I reply. "I hope to get lucky."

"You Americans are such bad boys," she says, not disap-
provingly. "Ray and I were just about to have a cocktail at the
bar. Will you join us?"

"I'd love to, except I'm only here until Monday and I'd
really like to see the lady I came here for."

Devi cocks her head, puzzled. "You're leaving tomorrow?"

"No, Monday."

"But today is Sunday."

"What happened to the international date line?" I ask
Ray.

Ray looks at me sheepishly. "Only works on the way home.
Turns out you actually lose a day getting here. My bad. Listen,
buddy—"

"Wait a minute. . . . I've only got, what, eighteen hours
here? Now I really have to find K."

Ray nods and looks like he's going to say more, but Devi
interrupts him. "K.? She's in our suite," she says. The change
to her smile is fractional, but transforms its message from be-
nevolence into something more mysterious. I can see why she
probably made an effective goddess.

"Suite," I say, shaking off her spell. "I like the sound of
that. What's the room number?"

"Surely you're not going to interrupt them."

"Them? What them?"

"Oh, it was quite magical," Devi says, now gushing like a
teenager. "Her boyfriend surprised her. He lined the hallway
with rose petals. . . ."

"Her boyfriend? K. doesn't have a . . . Nate is here?"

Ray shrugs. "I've been trying to tell you since you walked in."

"Nate is here. In fucking Korea? Lining the hallway with rose petals?"

"He was outside her room when she arrived," Devi continues, either divinely indifferent or just oblivious to my mortal suffering. "With his guitar. He has the voice of an angel. And the necklace . . ."

"There was a necklace?" I turn again to Ray. He looks back at me with a sympathetic cringe, as if he'd just seen me get kicked in the nuts.

"Diamonds," says Devi.

"*Diamonds?* As in plural?" My head is starting to spin. I feel like I might vomit.

"From Tiffany's," she chirps. "With the blue bag and everything!"

"Where are they now?" One look at Devi, and I can tell I sound as angry as I feel.

"In our suite," she replies, uncertainty creeping into her voice for the first time.

"The room number?" I ask, sounding even angrier. Devi's eyes flit nervously toward Ray. Threat assessment.

"You don't want to do that," Ray says, presenting a reassuring hand to my shoulder. I slap it away.

"What. Fucking. Room."

"I'm afraid I've said too much already," says Devi, clearly frightened by the look in my eyes. I focus on the small handbag she's now clutching to her chest. Pissed off enough to take on a goddess, I grab the purse out of her hands.

Devi shrieks. Ray looks caught between hugging me and socking me in the jaw. I root quickly through the bag, my hand emerging with her room key.

"Room 24021," I read aloud off the plastic tag. Replacing the key, I hand the bag back to her and storm toward the elevator. Or as close to it as I can, before a sumo wrestler stuffed into a security guard's uniform holds out an arm to block my way and asks to see my room key.

I pat my jacket as if looking for the key. The sumo has clearly seen this one before. "Guests only," he says.

"Have it your way." I walk back to the front desk. "I would like a room," I tell the clerk.

"So sorry," she says kindly. "All booked up."

"*Any* room."

"I'm so sorry. Perhaps I can recommend another hotel?"

"Listen," I say. "I have traveled almost seven thousand miles to see one of your guests."

"You're welcome to use the house phone," she says, her eyes flickering nervously toward the sumo. He begins walking over. I decide to accept the clerk's invitation to use the house phone.

I dial K.'s room. K.'s *suite.* After seven rings, someone picks up the receiver and—before either of us can say a word—hangs up.

I redial. This time it rings four times before I hear Nate's voice on the line.

"Whoever this is, fuck off!" he yells. *Click.*

I dial again. This time nobody picks up. I imagine Nate delighting K. as he rips the cord out of the wall, then jumps into bed to delight her some more. My head feels like it might explode.

"You okay, buddy?" asks Ray.

"What do you think?"

"Yeah, it's fucked up, I know. But I tried to warn you that night at the Western. Rock stars are like voodoo masters. I mean, look at Billy Joel. He's married to Christie Brinkley. *Christie Brinkley?* Are you shitting me?"

"Thanks, Ray. I feel so much better now."

"You need a drink."

"Your invitation still good?"

"I would, but Devi . . . I don't know if you made such a good impression." I spy the ex-goddess across the room. She stares back at me with dark fury. I quickly turn away. "Besides," Ray continues. "We were just about to get all funky and shit."

"Lucky you," I say, meaning it. I look at the clock on my pager. "I guess I can go feel sorry for myself for another seventeen hours."

"Dr. Ray has another idea. There's a place down the street. A youth hostel."

"A youth hostel?"

"Don't knock it until you've tried it, man. Youth hostels—this is an established fact—are full of horny sluts. Horny sluts on vacation from their better judgment. A good-looking guy like you gets laid with minimal effort, I mean *zero* rap, as long as you're cool with unshaved armpits and a lack of privacy."

My anger is slipping away, making room for sleep deprivation. "I don't know about the horny sluts, but I'm definitely pro-nap."

"There he is," Ray says, sounding relieved. "A little shut-eye, then you'll bang a slut. I recommend Australians. Find one with a friend and bang them both. Go root a couple of sheilas."

I pat Ray on the shoulder and exit the hotel. The valet appears immediately. "May I call you a taxi?"

I look up at the sky and see threatening clouds and approaching darkness. A perfect match to my mood.

"Thanks, but I'll walk."

I set out down a major thoroughfare that feels like New York, only with enviably wider sidewalks. Per Ray's directions to the youth hostel, I make a right turn at the first light and wind up, a block later, in a neighborhood with a much more suburban feel. A brightly illuminated 7-Eleven-type store anchors a stone-tiled public square surrounded by tenement-style buildings. The square itself is occupied by a few dozen Korean men, many in business suits, who gather in three distinct circles. Each circle has its own bottle of the local hooch, passed with cheery camaraderie from one smiling man to the next.

Not a female in sight, I notice. *That explains the smiles.*

16

"MY WIFE IS IN MANCHESTER, MY MIS-
tress in Hong Kong, and my lover in Ja-
karta," says the Englishman.

"You don't have a license to kill, do you?" I ask with sarcasm that goes unregistered.

The Englishman grins, his head snaking toward me. "No,
but I once saw a man die in my arms. What do you say to
that?"

"I think you're either totally full of shit or the most interesting man I've ever met," I reply. "But either way, I think
you've had a little too much of the yellow."

"Impossible!" he growls, rising to his feet. "I've been
drinking nothing but orange all night. Now let's go pull your
friend off that dancer before we're all led off in wristcuffs."

I'd met the Englishman, along with the Mormon and an
American woman who called herself Janie, at the Superior

Guesthouse, the hostel Ray recommended—a two-story wooden structure with a front door lit like a Christmas tree, hidden in a back alley between the ass-ends of a restaurant and a flower shop. The kind of place you can imagine the guidebook calling "an undiscovered gem."

I don't have a guidebook, and my discovery of the Superior is severely impeded by a blistering rain that begins right after I've passed the drinking circles. Coupled with darkness, visibility is a serious issue. I miss the entrance to the alleyway three times before stumbling inside, soaked and miserable.

The room can hardly be called a lobby after the Four Seasons—the small, wood-paneled cubicle has a lot more in common with a sweat lodge. I point toward the cheapest rate and am directed to a room with two bunk beds. Well-traveled backpacks claim dibs on the bottom bunks, so I climb onto the bed farthest from the door.

Sleep comes quickly, but it doesn't last long: Two hours later, I wake up shaking. Or rather the shaking wakes me up. I open my eyes to see Ray. He reeks of alcohol.

"You asleep, man?" he asks.

"I was. What are you doing here? Shouldn't you be having sex with a goddess right now? Getting all funky and shit?"

"Yeah, that one got kind of messed up."

"What happened to taking advantage of her low self-esteem?"

"Hah! Turns out part of the test for becoming a goddess was spending a night alone with a bunch of severed animal heads. Without crying. She was fucking three years old. Bitch is a natural-born icicle." Ray shivers for effect. "That, plus your going psycho didn't do me any favors."

"Sorry about that. I guess that makes us even for the whole international date line fuckup."

"You should be thanking me. Imagine if you had to spend the whole weekend here. Let's go get drunk. It's on me, motherfucker."

"What about us?" asks a British voice. We look over to see the Englishman, seated Indian style on the lower bunk across the room.

"I'd like to get drunk," chimes in a voice from the bunk below me. Ray jumps back from the bed, discovering the Mormon's head just inches from his crotch.

"Jesus Christ," says Ray. "Where the fuck did you come from?"

"Utah," replies the Mormon. "But that was a long time ago. Let's go get drunk."

Both men are clearly accustomed to being on the road. Each looks to be about thirty, with scruffy facial hair and billowy hippie clothes of indeterminate nationality. Neither has showered for several days.

"Where are we getting drunk?" says Janie, a big-boned but tragically low-waisted American girl with fashionable glasses. She's holding a manila envelope.

"Is that what I think it is?" says the Englishman, referring to the envelope. "Has our shipment from San Francisco arrived?"

"*My* shipment," Janie corrects him. "I know you're going

to try and treat this like your personal stash, but this is mine."

"What are you going to do with a whole sheet of acid?" asks the Mormon.

"Whatever I want," says Janie.

"Give us a taste, you sick tease," says the Englishman, springing to his feet.

Janie relents. "You can each have one tab." From the envelope she pulls out a letter-sized page scored into tiny boxes, each inked with a blue star. And, I gather, an ample serving of LSD. The Englishman and the Mormon hungrily accept their tiny tabs, placing them on their tongues. Janie turns to Ray and smiles. "Care to join us?"

"Me? No," says Ray. "I don't want to be seeing trails and shit when I'm forty."

"That's such an urban myth," she says, then turns to me. "What about you? You look like you could use a pick-me-up."

"Much appreciated," I say. "But I'd prefer to keep my feet on the ground just now. I believe there was some talk of getting drunk?"

"We could take them to Suzie's," suggests the Englishman. "How about it, mates? Shall we storm Hooker Hill?"

The word "hooker" seems to demolish any objection Ray might tender. A few minutes later, the five of us are packed into a taxi headed to Itaewon, Seoul's version of a red-light district. The Mormon—whose real name is Gene—uses the trip to explain how he's arrived at his current station in life. He'd been on a religious mission to Indonesia, with his wife and newborn daughter, when he experienced an "awakening."

The Englishman coughs theatrically. "More like a descent into moral disrepair."

"I just realized that I wasn't living the life I was supposed to be living," replies Gene.

"Because you're a queer," says the Englishman.

"I am not a queer," Gene says, looking directly at Ray. "Although this one's got this whole butch thing that's really turning me on."

"Because you're a goddamn *poofter*," the Englishman says, as if stating the obvious.

The Mormon smiles with practiced tolerance. "I'm really not gay. Anyway, I've been traveling for two years ever since. I've seen so much of the world."

"What about your family?" I ask.

"I tried to stay in touch with them at first. But after a while they didn't seem so interested in hearing from me. I think we're all just moving on."

When the taxi arrives at Suzie's, no one but Ray can find a wallet. Mine appears to have been stolen while I slept at the hostel. I take some consolation in the fact that the thief or thieves ignored my passport and plane ticket.

"The front desk should have warned you," Janie says. "That's the fifth or sixth robbery this week."

Ray grudgingly pays the cab fare. "He's got an excuse," he says, pointing to me. "What about the rest of you?"

The Englishman raises his hands in surrender. "What can

we say? We are but poor travelers. But if you're intent on recompense," he says, pointing to the Mormon, "I'm certain he'll bless your knob with a thorough spit-and-shine."

"Ha!" says the Mormon with a laugh. "He's kidding. I'm really not going to, you know, do what he said I'd do. That would be a sin." The Mormon's leg vibrates nervously: The acid is kicking in.

"Just pay the fare," Janie says. "And stop pretending that you don't like being the moneybags." Something tells me that Ray and Janie are not destined to be boon companions.

Inside, Suzie's looks like it might once have been a car dealership. Large plate-glass windows provide natural advertising to the foot traffic outside and a colorful view of the gaudily lit neighborhood for the customers within. Most of the interior space is devoted to a dance floor, where a dozen or so Korean beauties in slinky dresses and their male partners—the *clientele*, I assume—twirl incongruously to the sounds of New Kids on the Block. The scene looks more like a USO dance than a bordello: A large percentage of the men wear American military uniforms. "Yongsan Garrison's just west of here," Janie explains. "Thirty thousand red-blooded, shit-kicking United States Army men."

"How do the Koreans feel about that?" I ask.

Janie shrugs. "I guess they probably hate it. But not Suzie. Without them, she'd be out of business. Korean men are like totally straitlaced. They expect their women to be good little hausfraüs, dressed all conservative and staying home in the kitchen. If they saw Korean women acting this way, they'd go apeshit."

I look again at the dancers in search of behavior that might drive the locals crazy—public nudity, pussy-powered Ping-Pong balls, etc.—but I don't see much more than the occasional suggestive smile. As for the foreigners—Ray, in particular—the relatively demure dancing works like catnip. If the mention of hookers piqued Ray's interest, the sight of this many potential sexual partners of Asian descent has him bug-eyed. "How does this work?" he asks, bouncing from heel to heel.

"Miss Suzie will take care of us," says the Englishman.

Miss Suzie looks like an older version of one of her employees, although with Asian women I never can tell—my best guess at her age is somewhere between thirty and seventy. She addresses the Englishman with comfortable familiarity. "Welcome back, Mister Christopher. You bring friends tonight."

Miss Suzie leads us to a booth in the back. "I'll send someone over with your drinks." She pauses for a moment, carefully studying each of our faces. She bows gracefully and shifts her attention to another group, American soldiers who seem to be edging from boisterous toward rowdy.

"Shouldn't she have asked us what we wanted first?" I wonder aloud.

"There are only two drinks on the menu," says Mormon Gene. "Yellow and orange."

Gene is clearly tripping—the pupils of his eyes, as is the case with Janie and the Englishman, are as wide as saucers—but a couple of minutes later, one of the Korean beauties presents a tray bearing two plastic soda bottles, recycled and filled with what looks like radioactive Kool-Aid. Yellow and orange. "Grain alcohol," says Janie. "Be careful. This stuff will hit you like a brick wall."

Ray sneers at her. He grabs one of the disposable picnic cups that accompany the bottles, fills it with yellow, and chugs it down. Then he pours himself another.

Janie sneers back. "Ooooh!"

Ray ignores her. "So what now?" he asks.

"That's up to Miss Suzie," replies the Englishman. "But don't worry, you're in good hands."

When Miss Suzie reappears, she's holding hands with a dancer she's chosen, it seems, specifically for Ray. "This is Sunny," she says to him. "You look like a good dancer. She is very good dancer too."

Sunny, covered in a light layer of sweat from the dancing, smiles at Ray, not lewdly but like an innocent child being introduced to an adult. The effect on Ray is immediate. He throws back his second cup and in the same motion leaps to his feet and grabs Sunny's hand.

"You like Sunny?" asks Miss Suzie.

"I like Sunny," Ray replies, already leading her toward the dance floor. "Sunny days are here again."

"What about you, Mister Christopher? Mi-Hi always talk about you."

"That depends," the Englishman says, calling after Ray. "Mr. Moneybags! Are you paying for our dances too?"

Ray continues toward the dance floor without looking back, using the hand that isn't attached to Sunny to acquaint the Englishman with his middle finger. "I take that as a no," says the Englishman.

"Next time," says Miss Suzie.

"Except for the tragic-looking guy!" Ray yells back from the dance floor. "He gets whatever he wants!"

Miss Suzie turns to me. "He mean you?"

"No, not me."

"What kind of girl you like?"

"Right now? I don't know if I like girls at all right now."

She squints at me with a professional eye. "No. You like girls. Just wrong girls. Wrong girl."

"Impressive."

"I know," she says, holding my stare. "Don't worry. You find right girl. Maybe you dance with me tonight?"

"I'm flattered," I say. "In America, the men have to ask the women."

"So ask me, then. Go on. Your friend say it okay."

"Ask me after I've had another few of these," I say, raising my cup of yellow. She winks at me and moves on to another table. The Englishman, struck by a fit of acid-induced chattering, spends the next twenty minutes listing the pros and cons of maintaining intimate relations with three different women in three different countries. There seem to be a lot more cons, and I tell him so.

"You may be right," he says. "But we're men. What choice do we really have?"

Ray returns to the table once to drop off his belt pack and toss back an orange. The rest of the time, he and Sunny are the king and queen of this debaucherous prom. The Steve Winwood song on the speakers feels totally out of place, but that doesn't stop Ray from doing his *Saturday Night Fever* thing, lifting Sunny off the ground and spinning her around his shoulders. The soldiers applaud. Gene and the Englishman are too busily engaged in conversation to notice, a heated discussion over a secret worldwide conspiracy involving something called the Bilderberg Group. Janie's busy too, rooting through Ray's belt pack.

"What the fuck are you doing?" I ask.

Janie leaps back like I've slapped her. "Just, you know, looking. I'm sorry. I'm nosy."

"Did you take my wallet?"

"No." I examine Janie's face for signs of guilt. She stares back at me with LSD eyes, twin lumps of charcoal, burnt out and extinguished, a sarcastic reminder of K.'s radioactive blues.

We manage to finish the yellow and the orange and, after a mock parliamentary debate over the merits of each, order and drain another orange. We are thoroughly smashed, although to be honest, the three acid-trippers are handling their booze a lot better than Ray and me.

Ray finally staggers back to the table, a clearly delighted Sunny in tow. "Let's blow this clambake!" he yells. We're rising to our feet to go when the music screeches to a complete stop.

Conversations are abandoned mid-sentence. Someone draws thick black curtains over the plate-glass windows.

"What's going on?" I whisper to Janie.

"Military police," she whispers back.

"I thought this was all legal."

"American military. There's a curfew or something." I look over at the table of soldiers, currently subdued but ready to explode at any moment into laughter, violence, or both. A nervous glance at the Motorola tells me it's four in the morning: My return flight departs in only five hours. I mouth a silent prayer. *I do not want to be detained. Please God, let me make that flight.*

The patrol passes without further incident. The curtains reopen and the sound system springs back to life. Our momentum toward the door resumes as well. Ray hands a large wad of bills to Miss Suzie, who smiles at me on the way out.

"Maybe next time," she says.

I nod, too drunk to come up with anything clever.

We empty into the street. The rain has let up, but the streets still glisten. The air feels cleaner. The roads are nearly empty, save for a few scattered men passed out over the handlebars of their motor scooters, survivors of the drinking circles I'd witnessed earlier.

We move like a pack of wolves. Gene and the Englishman are the advance scouts, chasing each other down the streets with an energy verging on sexual, at least for Gene. Ray and Sunny are the alpha dogs, king and queen, still dancing down the street. Ray serenades her with an old song I half-recognize. *Sunny, thank you for the truth you let me see/Sunny, thank you for the facts from A to Z. . . .* Sunny, a stranger to our alphabet, basks in the attention. Janie and I make up the rear. At some point she loops her arm around mine. I don't stop her.

Gene breaks from his scouting and does a sort of jig in front of Ray and Sunny. He's grinning like a madman. "Am I going to see you two do some fuck-*ing*?"

"No you will fucking not, you goddamn fairy," replies Ray.

Gene giggles. "Maybe I'll trade beds with Chris. That way I'll be *riiight* beneath you."

I sense a shift in Ray's mood. "Back off, Gene," I say. "Mr. Moneybags doesn't have to rub elbows or any other parts of his body with our sorry asses. He's staying at the Four Seasons."

Ray stops as quickly as if he'd been punched in the gut. "Fuck."

"You're not staying at the Four Seasons?"

"Devi told me to cancel my room. 'Cause I'd be staying with her, right? Why waste all that money when I could be supporting some family of six in Nepal? Enough cow dung to last two winters . . . That *fucking bitch*!"

We idle for a while until the news settles in. The Englishman finally breaks the silence. "Bollocks," he says solemnly to Ray. "I guess Gene's going to get to see you fuck after all."

Sunny's face clouds with confusion, her disposition, for the first time tonight, at odds with her name. "How much farther is this place, anyway?" Ray barks at no one. "I'm getting a fucking cab." He drags Sunny toward an intersection with a higher concentration of motor traffic.

The Englishman catches up to them. "In all seriousness, mate, you're not going to bring her back to the hostel."

"Why not?" demands Ray.

"It's against the rules."

Ray reaches the intersection and flags a passing cab. "Fuck the rules." He guides Sunny into the car and looks at me. "Hurry up."

My arm is still intertwined with Janie's. I could let go and sprint toward the cab, were I that kind of asshole. Instead, I split the difference, half-jogging as fast as her little legs will allow. Gene and the Englishman interpret my drunken chivalry as an open invitation. They race toward the cab, piling in before we can.

The cabdriver glares skeptically at the six figures crammed in his backseat. He's even more concerned when we tell him we're going to the Superior Guesthouse. "You ditch fare," the driver says, his voice clearly singed by experience.

Ray searches for his wallet—no easy task, given the increasingly confused Korean hooker on his lap. "Seriously," the Englishman says. "Let Sunny out of the cab."

Gene, who'd beaten the Englishman into the car and earned the right to sit nearly on top of Ray, sounds his agreement. "He's right. It's against the rules. You should let her go." Gene grabs Sunny's chin between his fingers and speaks into her face. "You should go."

"Get your fucking hands off of her," says Ray, who has finally pried the wallet from his pocket. "I will break your goddamn fingers."

"You should let her go," says Gene.

Now Ray is screaming. "Where's my money?" He looks at me. I look at Janie. "Why are you looking at her?"

"I'm not."

Janie just stares out the window. "Mr. Moneybags spent it all at Suzie's," she says.

"She might be right," I say. "I saw you drop a lot of money back there."

"You should let her go," says Gene.

"You should shut the fuck up!" says Ray. I catch the driver's reflection in the rearview. He's obviously regretting his decision to pick us up.

"You don't even have any money," says Gene. "You should let her go."

Now the brakes are squealing. We're thrown forward by the momentum. The driver is yelling at us. "No money?!"

All eyes turn toward Ray. He opens his door and scoots out from underneath Sunny, dragging her behind him. The rest of us quickly join the exodus.

"I call police!" screams the driver, speeding away.

We're on a street that even in my short time in Seoul feels vaguely familiar—the major thoroughfare with the wide sidewalks. Janie renews her grip on my arm. "It's this way," she says, dragging me along.

I look over my shoulder at Ray, who has Sunny's hand in a

vise-grip. His bleary eyes bulge white with cartoonish panic. "What do you say, Ray?" I hear myself using a delicate voice, like a negotiator talking a jumper off a ledge.

"You should let her go," repeats Gene, and it's one time too many. Ray is spinning on one leg, dragging the other like a tetherball around a pole. There's a sickening crunch as his flying foot connects with the bridge of Gene's nose. Gene crumples to the ground, holding his face. Blood spurts out through his fingers.

Ray isn't finished yet. "I told you to shut the fuck up!" he yells. "But you couldn't shut up!" Ray kicks him again, this time in the ribs. The blow lifts Gene off the ground, several feet into a curb. Ray closes the distance.

I unspool from Janie and dive toward Ray, wrapping my arms around his waist and knocking him to the ground. I hold him there as he swings wildly, eager to continue the fight. We struggle for I don't know how long before I feel his body go limp, the anger fleeing like a vanquished spirit.

Gene sits on the edge of the sidewalk holding his ruined nose. The front of his shirt is stained red. Men in business suits, Monday morning commuters, emerge from a nearby subway terminal, surrounding Gene like water passing a pebble. Despite his condition only one man stops—across the street, to talk to a policeman. Both look back in our direction.

"Are you cool?" I ask Ray. "Because we really need to get out of here."

He nods weakly. I lift him to his feet and lead him toward

the entrance to the subway, the most obvious route of escape. We sprint down the steps into the terminal until turnstiles block our path. We pause to catch our breath. Sunny has for some mysterious reason chosen to follow us. She gestures at the turnstiles and says something in Korean, pointing toward a row of electronic vending machines built into the wall.

I snap at her like a condescending parent to a toddler in a tantrum. "No money. I know. You don't understand a word we're saying. *No. Money.*"

Sunny turns and walks away. Or so I think, until she accosts a man in a business suit. He brushes her away and she moves to another. I don't understand the words being exchanged, but begging looks the same everywhere. The men who don't ignore her offer an equally translatable expression—*shame,* a Korean girl so scandalously involved with two broke and broken white men. Until a stern-faced man with neatly combed white hair and wire-rimmed glasses hands her a few coins. Sunny clings to his sleeve, effusing until he pulls away in embarrassment.

Sunny returns from the vending machine with three tickets, handing one to me and pressing another into Ray's palm, which is as limp as the rest of him. She leads him by the arm toward the turnstile, guiding his ticket into the machine. She watches to make sure I do the same, then follows us onto the train. Luck is on our side: Ray has committed his almost certainly felonious assault above a subway line that happens to terminate at the airport. Sunny sits next to him, providing a shoulder for his slumping head.

We arrive at the airport three hours before my scheduled departure. "Breakfast," says Ray, the first words he's uttered since the fight.

"I thought you didn't have any money."

He pulls a green credit card out of his wallet. "American Express." He smiles weakly. "Don't leave home without it." The airport diner takes plastic. We drink a pot of coffee and sit in silence. Sunny, wearing sunglasses appropriated from Ray on the train, greedily devours a huge stack of pancakes.

At the entrance to customs, both Ray and Sunny hug me good-bye. I look back at them several times—despite the party clothes and the sunglasses, they remind me of that painting, the one with the farmer and his wife.

"Did you enjoy your trip?" asks the customs clerk.

"'Enjoy' isn't the first word that comes to mind. But it sure was interesting."

"How nice. Your luggage?"

"No luggage."

"No luggage?"

"What is it with you guys and the luggage? Can't someone just drop in for a visit?"

The clerk apprises me for a moment before returning to the paperwork in front of him. "It says your job is 'international businessman.' But you carry no briefcase?"

During happier times, maybe twenty hours ago, I'd written "international businessman" on my customs declaration card. A joke. "This was a social visit," I say, glancing at the teenage soldier with a machine gun who stands nearby. He looks a lot less like a teddy bear than yesterday's version. "I don't mean to sound impatient, but my plane is leaving very soon."

"Of course," the clerk says. "I just make one phone call first. Make sure you're not drug dealer." His smile doesn't reassure me. Why did I have to be such a smart-ass with the "international businessman" thing? What if they found the dope I flushed on the way over? Visions of strip searches and various tortures pass before my eyes. What if they make me take a lie-detector test, and ask me if I'm a drug dealer?

The clerk finally hangs up the phone and, after a pregnant pause, stamps my papers.

"I hope you enjoyed Korea."

17

DURING THE STEWARDESS'S MARCEL Marceau–like demonstration of the plane's emergency procedures, I cling to my seat with a white-knuckled grip that leaves indentations in the armrest. I'm almost positive that any minute Korean teenagers with automatic weapons are going to storm the plane calling my name. But once we're in the air, I relax enough to close my eyes.

I sleep for eight hours. I don't feel refreshed, exactly, but I'll settle for *improved*. I take stock of my situation. Broke. Brokenhearted. Mother sick and dying. I can almost hear the violins.

Let's get real, I say to myself. Hadn't I played a role in creating the unhappiness? Maybe Tana's right about karma. Did I really expect any favors from the universe after shamelessly exploiting my mother's illness to get a plane ticket?

When my plan from the beginning was to steal another guy's girl?

I remember, during one of my father's state-mandated alcohol awareness programs, he was asked to make a list of the people he'd done wrong while under the influence. It's time to get my own house in order. I ask one of the stewardesses for a pen and paper.

1. **Mom.** Gave me everything; rewarded her by fleeing the ranch as soon as I could. Deceived her about job, accepting gifts and admiration under false pretenses. She's sick and dying in a hospital bed, a condition I exploited to chase a girl halfway around the world.

2. **Tana.** My best friend, my sister from another mother—so how could I have been so blind to her feelings? Answer: I'm a jackass.

3. **Daphne.** Sure, she's crazy, but how much of that is my fault? Cheated on her and lied about it. Provoked arguments and fueled fires. Made her feel wrong, even when I knew I wasn't right. I even stole her fantasy about the Chelsea Hotel and made it my own. Supposed to be helping her find her father; instead pursuing sex with supermodels.

4. **K.** Tried to sabotage her relationship for no other reason than my own libido. Took advantage of breakup and rebound.

5. Nate. See #4.

6. Herman. Lied about poetry.

7. Zach Shuman. Assistant manager at Hempstead Golf and Country Club. Still a prick. But I got him fired. Worse, I was happy to get him fired. What does that say about me?

8. The kid in my freshman hall whom I sprayed in the face with a fire extinguisher while tripping on mushrooms. Shouldn't have done it. Damn: I don't even remember his name.

I KEEP SCRIBBLING FOR SEVERAL pages, amazed at how many long-forgotten slights I'm able to dig up. The last one turns out to be the most shocking:

27. Dad.

DAD. THERE'S PROBABLY NOT A wrong in the world I don't blame you for. Fine, you're never going to win a "Father of the Year" award, but you put a roof over my head and paid for my education, gifts I've accepted with a big *Fuck You*. Somehow I've turned you into the Antichrist, when in truth you're simply just as lost and stupid and confused and flawed as everybody else.

When the plane lands at Kennedy, I call Billy—collect, given the loss of my wallet—to tell him I was stuck at the airport without money or means to get into the city.

"I'll get someone to cover," says Billy. "But you and the personal days, kid. It's getting to be a real issue."

"My bad. Extenuating circumstances."

"Spare me the ten-dollar words. I'll be straight with you. You've brought in a lot of extra business these last few weeks. Don't think he hasn't noticed." Billy's referring to the half-dozen characters I'd created to service Danny Carr's smoking needs, characters now facing retirement. "You've earned a little goodwill. But goodwill is a checking account. And you're coming close to being overdrawn."

"Understood, Billy."

"Good. Now hurry the fuck up."

"There isn't anybody who could give me a ride, is there?"

Billy hangs up the phone.

I think about calling Tana, but I haven't spoken to her since our dinner. There's only one real option. After some confusion with a receptionist unfamiliar with receiving collect calls, I'm connected to my father.

"Hey, it's me," I say. "I need a ride."

"Are you okay? Where are you?" He almost sounds concerned.

"The airport."

"What are you doing at the airport?"

"I'd rather not say."

A few seconds pass in silence. "You know I just got into work."

"What an amazing coincidence. I just dialed these digits, completely at random, and found you at the office. Come on,

Dad. I wouldn't be calling you unless it was my option of last resort. Which it is."

"Kennedy or La Guardia?"

"Kennedy. International Terminal. And not to sound ungrateful, but if you could find it in your heart to repay me that hundred you 'borrowed' from me, this would be a good time."

He arrives an hour later. I climb into the passenger seat.

"You okay?" he asks.

"I'm fine. Let's go."

Dad stops staring at me long enough to look into his side mirror. He pulls away from the curb. "Is this drugs? Are you into drugs?"

"I'm not on drugs."

"Good." He punches the dashboard lighter and pulls his cigarettes out of his pocket. "You want one?"

"Yes please." I'd smoked my last Camel somewhere over the Pacific Ocean. My father hands me the pack and, when the lighter clicks, gestures for me to light mine first.

"It's actually about a woman," I say.

"I'm sorry to hear that."

"That I'm into women?"

"That you're shaping up to be as big a dope as I am."

"Don't sell yourself short," I say with a smile. "You've left me with big shoes to fill."

"Heh," he sputters. "Listen. Your mom's not doing so well."

"I know. I know I've haven't been so good about visiting, but I'm going to be better here on out."

"Here on out's not that long, is all I'm saying. Do we have an actual destination?"

"Train station, assuming you have my money."

"I have your money. So where the hell were you, anyway?"

I bring him up to speed, or try to. The story has just reached Hooker Hill when we reach the station.

"Guess we'll finish it another time," he says, handing me a hundred bucks. "Maybe over a couple of drinks."

"I'd like that."

"I'm sorry for being such a dick."

"You aren't a dick. And I haven't always been the best son, either."

"Visit your mother," he yells after me as I walk away.

I make it into the city in time to put in a half-day of work, and I've got enough money to return to the Island that evening. My father proves to be a master of understatement. My mother is barely conscious when I walk into her hospital room, doped up on serious meds that at any other time I might have coveted. She smiles when she sees me, but can't quite muster the energy to speak. I've been sitting with her for an hour when I see Dr. Best pass by in the hallway. I chase him down.

"She doesn't look that good," I say.

"You're going to have to remind me who you are again. . . ." I do. "Right!" says the doctor. "I thought we already talked about this?"

"Maybe with my father?"

"Right! So no, not good. Maybe a week or two."

"A week or two?"

He crinkles his eyes into a face he probably learned at med school on the day they studied Dealing with Terminal Patients and Their Families. "I wish we could have done more. I'm sure she appreciates you being here. Even when they can't respond, like she can't, they still appreciate it. That's what they say, anyway." I realize for the first time that he's shaking my hand.

I spend the night in her room, listening to her breathe until I fall asleep in a chair. I repeat the same ritual for the rest of the week, waking up in the chair each morning, catching the train, and filing in and out of the city like the rest of the clock-punchers. Each night I return to my bedside vigil, watching my mother slip closer and closer to the finish line.

18

"AT LEAST SHE DIDN'T SUFFER LONG," says Dottie, apparently disregarding the twenty-two years my mother was married to my father, who seems as numb and detached during her funeral as he'd been during her life. Not that anyone shows much life during the solemn and humorless service. My dad's temperament or lack thereof matches the demeanor of my mom's stoic relations, several of whom have flown in from the Midwest.

The obvious exception to the emotional void is Tana, an absolute wreck before, during, and after the service. When the service ends, she grabs me in a hug. "I'm so sorry," she says.

"Walk with me while I smoke," I say. By unspoken agreement my father and I have avoided lighting up in front of my mother's family, so as not to remind them of the lung cancer that killed their nonsmoking relation.

"It's weird," I say upon reaching a thicket of trees that offers some privacy. "I think I always saw her as a two-dimensional character—you know, *Mom*. She lived a whole life inside of her mind that I never gave her credit for. That I'll never know. I guess it's true what they say: We all die alone."

"What the hell is wrong with you guys?" Tana asks.

"That depends on what you mean by 'you guys.'"

"Men. You all say the same stupid shit. 'The world is meaningless. We all die alone. Nothing means anything.'"

"If anything meant anything," I say, "my mother wouldn't have died of somebody else's disease."

"My point is that she didn't die *alone*," says Tana, staring at the mourners filing out of the cemetery. "Maybe we're all out there, floating by ourselves in some big black void. But we build connections, you know? We build our own worlds with the people we love. Your mom didn't die alone. She had friends and she had family, and even when they let her down, she always felt like she had a home."

Tana is bawling again. I hug her again. "I'm sorry," I whisper into her ear.

"Me too," she replies. "But let's not fucking dwell on it."

I hold Tana tight, two lone figures surrounded by trees.

19

A FEW DAYS LATER, I RETURN TO THE Chelsea Hotel for what will be the last time. I skirt past Herman without his noticing me and sprint upstairs to my room. The locks have been changed.

"Deh you ah," says Herman when I return to the lobby.

"Hi. I seem to be having some trouble with my key."

"Ya seem ta have a little trubble widda rent as well."

"Yeah, about that . . ."

"I also tawkt to a friend at the *New Yawkah*. Dey nevah hudda ya." Herman grins and holds up his key ring. Except instead of leading me upstairs, he unlocks a supply closet behind him. My duffel and typewriter are inside. "Tanks fah stayin' widdus. Besta luck widda poetry."

I'm lugging my stuff through the front door when Nate holds it open for me. "Weed Man!" he yells. "Where the hell have you been?" I look at K., who's standing next to him. She seems more interested in something on the floor. "You're not leaving us, are you?"

"Moving out," I say.

"Well, good luck and all that."

K. finally speaks. "We should buy you a drink."

"I can't, baby," says Nate. "I told that reporter-ess from *Rolling Stone* I'd call her back an hour ago. What time is it, anyway?"

"Well then *I* should buy you a drink," says K.

K. and I wander into the restaurant next door. Just a month ago, it was the birthplace of our relationship; now it will host our postmortem. "What happened to you?" she asks as the drinks arrive.

"I went to Korea to see you."

Her blue eyes play emotional hopscotch, starting on confusion, then bouncing through guilt, remorse, and sadness before returning to the starting point. "You came to Korea? Why didn't you . . ."

"Nate."

She looks back at the floor. "I swear to you I had no idea he was going to be there. He just, you know, showed up."

"With a lot of flowers, I'm told. And jewelry." My eyes dart toward a string of diamonds sparkling around her neck.

"This is my fault," she says. "I think I might have given you the impression that Nate and I . . . that things were a lot more settled than they were."

"You think?"

"I know. I feel horrible. We were . . . You were great. You *are* great and you deserve so much—"

I hold up a hand to stop her. "First of all, spare me the breakup speech. I've delivered enough of them to know how you're feeling."

"You don't know how I'm feeling. . . ."

"Second, I have to say, I kind of got what I deserved."

She pauses before continuing. "I was just so confused. And then when I got back, you were gone. No note, no phone call."

"It's been a little crazy."

"Your mom?" she asks. I nod and leave it at that. K. looks at me sympathetically. "You must hate me."

"I don't hate you," I reply, mostly meaning it. "So how about Nate? *Rolling Stone*? He's the real deal."

"Maybe. For now. Who knows what the future might bring?" I can see she's opening the door for me. Offering me a glimmer of hope.

"Who knows?"

We hug good-bye. I struggle with the bag and the typewriter for a block before setting both down in an alleyway. I walk to the station empty-handed and catch the first train back to Levittown.

20

I COMMUTE TO WORK FROM THE ISLAND for a couple of weeks, until I'm summoned by the Pontiff to the apartment on the Lower East Side. He tells me that it's a downturn in the economic climate, maybe just seasonal, and that business is dropping for all of the Faces. But he's got a copy of the *Post* open next to him, a lurid story detailing the first day of the *State of New York v. Daniel Carr*, and I know the real reason why I'm being fired. I love the Motorola too much to smash it against the stairwell, so I hand it to Billy on the way out.

My father and I turn out to be pretty good housemates, in that we stay out of each other's way and keep the place relatively clean. We're too sad or superstitious to smoke inside anymore, so instead we fill coffee cans with butts outside, near the part of the house that remains scorched from Daphne's adventure with fire.

I visit her a few days later. She's finally trimmed the dye out of her hair, which has grown down to her shoulders. Her eyes, which moisten with tears when I tell her about my mother, have regained their sparkle. When my own eyes burst like a dam, she holds me and whispers in my ear, "It's all going to be okay."

When I finally pull myself together, she escorts me to the front entrance. "They think I'm getting better," she says. "Do I have them fooled or what?"

"Does that mean the institutional phase of your life is coming to a conclusion?"

"This week's episode, anyway." Her sense of humor is back: It's the same old Daphne. I remember what it was like to fall in love with her. How the few years' difference in age had seemed like a great mystery to be unraveled. She introduced me to the Ramones and Jonathan Richman and to parties that lasted for three days. To sex in semipublic places. To the idea that love and pain often go hand-in-hand. I'd been naïve when I met her, an eighteen-year-old kid cocksure and maybe a little happier for it. I'd never be that person again. But now, looking at Daphne, I can see that kid reflected in her eyes.

"I might get out by the end of the month," she says. I hug her good-bye and tell her to call me at home as soon as she knows.

A few days later, my dad moves out of the house. "It's Janine," he says. "She won't sleep in your mother's bed. Like she's going to catch cancer from a bed. Dizzy broad, that one."

"The best ones always are."

"Anyway, she finally left that drip she's married to, and we were thinking about getting an apartment together. Actually, we *did* get an apartment together."

"Congratulations."

"You can stay here as long as you want. I'm not planning on selling—not now, anyway, with real estate in the tank. Maybe you can contribute a little when you start working again."

"Thanks, Dad. I know it's weird, but I honestly hope you and Janine are happy together."

"Happy," he says with a snort. "No one ever said it was about being happy."

21

FOR THE FIRST COUPLE OF WEEKS after she returns to college, Tana and I speak on the phone almost every night. But after a couple of weeks, the calls evolve into something shorter, less frequent, and decidedly more upbeat—a side effect, I suspect, of a guy named Todd she's started seeing.

"Gay?" I venture, during one of the times we are actually able to connect.

"He's really into the Waterboys," Tana admits. "But I'm happy to say that he otherwise seems to display all the necessary characteristics associated with a red-blooded man."

"You little vixen," I say. "You're getting laid."

I can't see her, but I know she's blushing. "So tell me about your new job," she says.

With no job and no girlfriend, I'd poured my focus into the house, specifically the walls and carpets still charred by

Daphne's attempted arson. It was during one of my trips to the hardware store that I ran into Zach Shuman, my former boss at the Hempstead Golf and Country Club, who'd been fired for my misdeeds. Surprisingly, he looked at me without anger.

"Heard about your mom," said Zach. "Fucked up."

"I know. Thanks."

"You know I'm managing Beefsteak Charlie's over in Garden City," he said. "I could use a waiter."

My mother's final gift to me, I chuckled to myself as I donned slacks and a tuxedo shirt a few days later.

A couple of weeks into the new job, Daphne calls. "Guess who's escaping the loony bin?" The day she's released, I pick her up in my mom's Buick.

"Where to?" I ask.

"Someplace with a noncommunal shower," says Daphne. I take her back to my house. As we pull up, I see her examining the exterior for signs of fire damage, but I've done a pretty good job with the paint. Inside, she eyes the bathroom (recently retiled and regrouted) like a castaway might view a steak. She doesn't come out for an hour. I finally muster the courage to knock, steeling myself to the possibility that she might not be as well as she claimed.

Daphne opens the door, dripping wet and totally naked. "I forgot to ask you for a towel," she says. We fall into each other's arms, kissing hungrily. Despite some trepidation on her part—"The fluoxetine is supposed to affect my libido," she warns—everything still fits where it should. We spend the night in my parents' bed, a practice that continues without interruption each night that follows. I bring her with me to the Kirschenbaums for Passover dinner.

My father arrives with Janine, who shows no signs of defrosting despite a warm embrace from the collective crowd. But the mood is festive, with much of the focus on Todd, Tana's guest from school. Despite some residual teenage acne, Todd seems very much to be what older folks call an "upstanding young man." More important, he seems intensely devoted to Tana and maybe untainted by whatever baggage haunts the rest of us. The room is swarming with so many good vibes that Dad embraces Daphne, never mentioning the fire. "Break it up!" yells Uncle Marvin when the hug goes on a little too long.

Rounding out the dinner is a late arrival, one Henry Head, accompanied by a Mrs. Head. The private investigator takes me aside shortly after the second glass of wine.

"I've been trying to get in touch with you," says Head. "But that phone number you gave me doesn't work no more." The Motorola. "No skin off my knee," he continues. "I just had some news for you, is all. I was at this garage sale with Lorna." He gestures toward Mrs. Head. "I found this old phone book. They were trying to sell an old phone book, can you believe it? What good is an old phone book?"

"You tell me."

"A lot of good, as it turns out. I remembered that name

you gave me, Peter Robichaux. You ever read any James Lee Burke? He's got a detective named Dave Robicheaux. From New Orleeeens."

I shake my head no. Daphne, hearing her father's name spoken aloud, joins us to hear the rest.

"Anyway, would you believe the bastard, pardon my French, was in the book? Emphasis on 'was,' because like I said, old phone book. But I took a drive out there anyway, just to see."

"You found him?"

"No. Moved out years ago. But the current resident said he still got mail from Kings Park. You know, the state cuckoo facility? My guess is he was a resident there for a while." I sneak a glance at Daphne, looking for some reaction to the idea that she and her father share the same institutional alma mater, but her face reveals nothing.

"Anyway," Head continues, "I did some checking. He did some time at Bellevue, schizophrenia and all that, in the early eighties. Until Reagan came in and kicked 'em all out onto the curb. I'm afraid that's where the path gets cold."

"You check for a rap sheet?" asks Marvin, who has snuck up on the conversation unnoticed.

"Check," replies the detective. "But no dice."

"Huh," Marvin says.

Daphne doesn't seem interested in pursuing it further, but as we drive home from the seder, I figure it's worth double-checking.

"We could hire a different detective," I suggest. "Maybe one with half a brain."

"Maybe I'm not supposed to find him," she says, without apparent emotion. "Things happen for a reason, you know?"

So we return to our lives. I work plenty of shifts at the restaurant; she finds a job at a record store. While I would never have pegged either of us for homebodies, we're happy in our new roles. We shop for groceries, share the yardwork and bills, hold hands when we go to the movies. When Uncle Marvin calls, a week later, to tell me that he's found him, I have to ask who.

"Robichaux," says Marvin. "Who the fuck else would I be talking about?"

22

EASTER SUNDAY—THE DAY WE'VE chosen for our voyage—could be a commercial for springtime: There's blue sky and sunshine to spare. We pile into my mom's car, compromising on the Rolling Stones for a sound track as we rumble down the 495.

In the weeks that followed my mother's death, I tended to associate any thoughts of the city with a gnawing, reptilian sense of dread. But today, my lady riding shotgun and a mystery almost solved, I feel energized. Some of this, admittedly, might have to do with the clouds of fragrant smoke emanating from Uncle Marvin in the backseat. Both Daphne and I decline his offers to share, me for safety reasons, her because, she says brightly, "I want to be sober for this."

Following the conversation at Passover, Uncle Marvin, claming that "Henry Head couldn't find a Jew in the Bronx," had taken it upon himself to make a few inquiries. He struck paydirt when he ran Peter Robichaux's name past an old friend in the city's Fifth Precinct, an area extending from Chinatown and Little Italy to the East River. After some more digging, Marvin's friend turned up the arrest, one year earlier, of a local vagrant named "Peter Robishow." The charge was misdemeanor assault, but the crime itself—spitting on a police officer—wasn't quite heinous enough to impress the judge, who ordered him released without a trial.

"Robishow" had no address. Marvin's buddy hooked us up with Reuben Brown, a homeless rights advocate in the area. Uncle Marvin cannot say "homeless rights advocate" without visible scorn. "They don't have jobs or responsibilities and we feed 'em all the cheese they can eat," Marvin says. "What the hell more rights do they want?" We decide that it's best for me to call Reuben.

I tell Reuben that Robichaux—whom he calls "Robes"— might be in line for an inheritance. Reuben doesn't look convinced by my story, but agrees to meet us in a spot underneath the Brooklyn Bridge on the condition that we help him distribute a few dozen loaves of day-old bread to the people who live there.

"I just want to remind you," says Reuben, a light-skinned black man with red hair, "that most of these folks ain't right in the head. Don't get your hopes too high, is all I'm saying."

"Understood!" says Daphne. Reuben nods slowly, taken aback by her enthusiasm to blast full throttle into the makeshift village in front of us, a collection of cardboard boxes, shopping carts, and rancid blankets. Despite the loaves of bread, most of their occupants hide when they see us coming. The ones brave enough to look us in the eye do so with suspicion.

"He lives in a box?" Daphne asks Reuben, saying "box" as if it could have been "brownstone" or "Dutch Colonial."

"Robes? No, Robes lives *down under*."

"Great," Marvin says. "A goddamn Mole Man."

"What's a Mole Man?" I ask.

"It's an urban myth," says Reuben. "A lot of these men and women, they've got no choice but underground. An old subway tunnel is a hell of a lot warmer than a refrigerator box. Somehow the story got started that they got their own society, with rules and laws and such. Their own civilization, if you will. But I'll tell you from experience, it ain't so. Ain't nothing civilized about living in a subway tunnel."

Still, it's hard not to imagine, descending into the darkness of a tunnel, that we're entering a lost kingdom. We're definitely being watched—more than once I catch a glimpse of white eyes against the gloomy pitch. I find Daphne's hand, figuring she could use the reassurance, but she seems calm and happy. We could be going on a picnic. I chalk it up to effective medication.

"Is it much farther?" asks Daphne.

"Just around the bend," Reuben replies. He's carrying a giant aluminum flashlight, waving it at the rats that cross our path. A sudden rumbling sound shakes the walls and straightens the hairs on the back of my neck. It turns out to be a passing subway train.

"Hey, Robes, you in there?" says Reuben, aiming the flashlight's beam through a separation in the wall. "It's me, Reuben." There's a reply, a cross between a grunt and a wail, that encourages Reuben to continue. "I got some friends with me. Friends of *yours*, they say."

My eyes accustom to the room's low light, and I can make out what looks like a human figure crumpled against the wall. Daphne approaches him slowly, one hand raised as if to touch him. "Dad," she says. "It's me. Daphne."

"Dad?!" Reuben exclaims. "You didn't tell me nothing about that."

"Shush," says Marvin, who's sparking up a joint. Reuben refuses his offer to share.

I rest a hand on Daphne's shoulder. She brushes it away, moving toward the figure on the floor. "Dad," she repeats. The figure twitches, struggling to face her. It's impossible to read the expression on his face, if there is one: Reuben is careful not to shine his light directly into the man's eyes.

"Dad," she says. "Is that you?"

The figure whispers something unintelligible. Daphne continues to edge closer. I can sense Reuben stirring uneasily behind me.

Daphne's bringing her hand to the figure's face. "Be careful, Daph," I warn, without any comprehension whatsoever of what the risks might be. Daphne removes something shiny from her pocket and squeezes it, creating a vaguely familiar noise, like a beer can being crushed. When Reuben swings the flashlight toward them, I see that Daphne's holding the bottle of lighter fluid I use to maintain my Zippo.

"What the fuck?!" says Reuben. Now Daphne's holding a book of matches, flinging one at the crumpled mess on the floor. The pile erupts in flames.

I grab at her from behind. Her arms flail wildly. Uncle Marvin takes a more direct approach, stamping out the fire. Daphne rewards him for his heroism with a sharp kick to the testicles, or what might have been testicles if Uncle Marvin still had them. Instead there's a pop as she connects with Marvin's colostomy bag, which explodes like a piñata.

The figure on the floor, still smoldering, rises and runs away. The flames spread quickly through the room. "We gotta get out of here," says Marvin, struggling to his feet. He hobbles back the way we'd entered. Reuben and I drag Daphne after him.

It's too dark to see the smoke pouring through the tunnels, but we're choking on it. "Keep moving," yells Marvin. I follow Reuben's lead, helping to drag Daphne toward a pinpoint of light in the distance. The light gets brighter as we reach the entrance.

The scene outside is mayhem. Dozens of people, faces blackened by soot, follow the smoke out of the subway tunnel into the makeshift village. Reuben is struggling with Daphne, assaulting her with a flurry of profanities that continues long after I've shoved a few twenties into his hand. Daphne curls into a fetal ball on the ground. Marvin stands nearby tending to his ruined groin.

I scan the chaos for some sign of Robes. But all I can see is an army of charred zombies, coated in soot, grime, piss, and blood, blinking their eyes against the bright sun.

23

DAPHNE REMAINS NEARLY COMATOSE for the entire drive home. After we drop Marvin off, I drag her into the shower, do my best to scrub her clean, and tuck her into bed.

"What about the farewell drugs?" are her only words to me, a line from *Sid and Nancy*. Then she falls asleep, so deeply she snores.

I spend most of the night sitting in a chair next to the bed, watching her. I doze off at some point during the early hours of the morning. When I wake, the bed is empty and the Buick is gone from the driveway. There's a note pinned to the refrigerator: "Sorry."

The call from Kings Park arrives later that afternoon. *Miss Robichaux has decided to check herself back in*, says a bored administrator whose greatest concern is that I pick the Buick up from the parking lot.

The next morning, another spectacularly sunny day, my father drops me off at the institution. Daphne shuffles out into the visiting area, looking very much like she did the first time I saw her there. She speaks slowly. They've clearly upped her dosage.

"So," she asks. "How do you like me now?"

"Same as it ever was," I say. "You look like the woman I love."

She smiles weakly. "You know why love stories have happy endings?" I shake my head. "Because they end too early," she continues. "They always end right at the kiss. You never have to see all the bullshit that comes later. You know, *life*."

"Lady, this love story is just beginning. Rest up, because when you're feeling better . . ." I pause, because I don't know exactly what to say next.

"What?" she asks. "We go back to the suburbs? We get married? That's us, right? Two and a half kids and a white picket fence."

"Fuck all that. We can move back into the Chelsea. I'll even pick you up in a big yellow taxi." It's a reference to the end of *Sid and Nancy* that I hope will cheer her up.

"You're not Sid," she says, shuffling back to her room.

Daphne's words sting at first, mostly because she's right. All of the bourgeois bullshit that we used to make fun of— stupid jobs and suburban values—has somehow become my life. I'm beginning to understand her urge to set fire to the world.

But I'm not Sid Vicious. Despite the world being a fucked-up place, well past fixing, I don't have any desire to wreck the joint.

Maybe it's just the sunshine that socks me in the face when I walk out the door, but I'm just not ready to go home and get ready for work. I could start fresh. Find a job in a better restaurant. Quit food service altogether.

I don't even have to stay in New York. K. said that traveling was lonely, but I've never even been to California, where the sun's supposed to shine like this every day of the year.

I pop a cassette into the Buick's stereo. It's the Ramones. I turn the volume up high and roll down the windows. The highway air tastes of fumes, but it still feels goddamn good to breathe.

ACKNOWLEDGMENTS

This book never would have existed without my follicularly challenged agent Charlie Runkle, the best in the business. Thanks also to his foxy wife Marcy, for everything she does to keep him that way. I also owe a huge debt of gratitude to my editor, Cara Bedick, whose quiet persistence saved you, dear reader, from many a cliché (although maybe not this one).

To Tom K., for believing in me before anybody else did. Thanks also, in no particular order, to Alex Cox, Sid Vicious and Nancy Spungen (and Gary Oldman and Chloe Webb), the very helpful staff at Kings Park, Johnny's Deli and their life-sustaining egg sandwiches, Randy Runkle, the Ramones, and Judy Blume, who taught me everything I think I know about women.

Finally, I am grateful to my family: my father, for observing early (and often) that I wasn't cut out for doing honest work; my sisters, whose laughter at the dinner table still keeps me going; and my mother, to whom I owe, literally and metaphorically, absolutely everything.